Kerry pushed past him and walked up the short, steep ramp and into the trailer. "It *is* her," she said softly as she stared at the frightened horse that was trying desperately to back away.

"*Who?*" Holly demanded loudly.

"The old man's chestnut mare. I've found her."

"Have you two finished gawking at my horse?" the man asked impatiently.

"I've got to buy her," Kerry whispered urgently.

Holly stared first at the neglected horse, then at her friend's determined expression. "But *why?* She looks ten times worse than the cow-faced one."

"Because if I don't, she'll end up in a can of dog food."

BEST FRIENDS

IF WISHES WERE HORSES

BY MAGGIE DANA

ILLUSTRATIONS BY DONNA RUFF

Troll Associates

To Jamie

Library of Congress Cataloging in Publication Data

Dana, Maggie.
    If wishes were horses.

    (Best Friends; #4)
    Summary: Kerry rescues a mistreated horse from a
grisly fate and trains her for the upcoming horse
show, unaware that the horse may be stolen.
    [1. Horses—Fiction]   I. Ruff, Donna, ill.
II. Title.   III. Series: Best friends (Mahwah,
N.J.); #4.
PZ7.D194If   1988   [Fic]   87-16201
ISBN 0-8167-1197-6 (lib. bdg.)
ISBN 0-8167-1198-4 (pbk.)

A TROLL BOOK, published by Troll Associates,
Mahwah, NJ 07430

Copyright © 1988 by Troll Associates, Mahwah, New Jersey
Printed in the United States of America.

10   9   8   7   6   5   4   3   2   1

Chapter One

The letter was waiting for her when she came into her bedroom, propped up in front of the lamp on her bedside table. Liz must have put it there and forgotten to tell her about it.

Kerry ran her hand through her dark brown hair and stared at the envelope. It had been mailed from Saudi Arabia over a week ago. She'd been expecting a letter from her father any day. But now that it had finally arrived, she wasn't sure she wanted to open it. Finally her curiosity got the better of her, and she snatched the letter off the table and ripped it open.

"Dear Kerry," her father had written. "This will have to be a quick letter, and I hope you won't be upset when I tell you that I won't be coming home until sometime this fall.

"I know you're worried about where we're going to live when my job is finished, but I'm afraid I can't tell you any more than I did the last time I wrote.

We may end up back in our old home in Connecticut, or I may be sent overseas again. I've written to Liz Chapman, thanking her for taking care of you. I've asked her if you can stay with them till I get back. As soon as I know what our future plans are going to be, I'll write or phone. Take care. Love, Dad."

Kerry gave a loud sigh and dropped the thin airmail sheet onto the bed. It wasn't quite what she'd been expecting, but at least she had more time at Timber Ridge with the Chapmans. She secretly wished she could live at Timber Ridge forever, but she knew it was impossible. Once her father got back from the Middle East, she'd have to move back to Connecticut, at least for a little while, until his next job. And then? No one knew.

While her father was away, Kerry had come to stay with her aunt in Vermont. But after only two weeks in Aunt Molly's tiny apartment, Kerry had gotten bored and taken a job as a companion to fourteen-year-old Holly Chapman. Holly's mother, Liz, ran the Timber Ridge Stables.

Kerry smiled as she thought about Holly, her best friend. When she'd first arrived at Timber Ridge, Holly had been confined to a wheelchair. She couldn't walk because of a car accident that had occurred two years before. Her father was killed and she was left paralyzed.

Holly's paralysis was considered a hysterical paralysis, so there was always a chance that she might walk again. And she had. She was almost fully healed now.

"Hey, Kerry, come here!" Holly yelled from the bedroom next door.

Kerry pushed her father's letter from her mind and hastily slipped on a pair of clean shorts. She went into Holly's bedroom. "What's up?" she asked Holly, who was sitting cross-legged on her unmade bed, surrounded by magazines and newspapers.

Holly shuffled around in the messy newspapers. "Ah-ha!" she cried as she pounced on a torn sheet of newsprint. "Here it is. Listen to this. 'Red roan mare, sixteen hands, good jumper, no vices, owner going to college . . .'"

Kerry stifled a giggle. Holly just wouldn't give up! Ever since Kerry had confided in her that she wanted to buy a horse, Holly had drowned both of them with "horse for sale" advertisements. "I *hate* roans," Kerry said with a sour expression. "Who wants to ride a 'pink' horse?"

"Beggars can't be choosers," Holly said flippantly, and started looking through the newspaper again.

Kerry flinched. Holly wasn't kidding. All she had to spend on the horse of her dreams was the seven hundred dollars she'd earned that summer.

"Here's a good one," Holly muttered. "'Gray gelding, five years old, shown successfully last season.'" She stopped and frowned. "Uh-oh. No good. They want two thousand dollars for him."

Kerry groaned. She was starting to think that Liz and Holly had been right when they'd told her she couldn't possibly buy a decent horse with only seven hundred dollars. All the horses that sounded promising were too expensive, and the ones she could afford were either too young, too old, or too small!

While Holly rustled through the pile of newspa-

3

pers, Kerry wondered what her father's reaction was going to be when he found out she was buying a horse. If she forced herself to be sensible about it, she knew it wasn't a very smart move. Their future plans were up in the air. Where would she keep a horse if they were constantly on the move?

"This one's *perfect*!" Holly cried out suddenly. "'Bay mare, excellent jumper, seven years old, perfectly sound. Only six hundred and fifty dollars.'"

"Wow!" Kerry shrieked, and snatched the newspaper away from her friend. "Where is it? I want to read it myself."

Holly pointed toward the bottom of the page.

Kerry's face fell as she read the advertisement. "You dummy," she said affectionately. "It's only twelve hands high!"

"Whoops," Holly said, giggling. "I guess I missed that."

"I'll never find anything," Kerry wailed.

"You can always share Magician with me," Holly offered when she saw her friend's miserable expression.

"Thanks, but it's not quite the same as having my own horse," Kerry replied quietly. She was very grateful for the offer because she loved riding Holly's big black horse, Magician. But now that Holly was healthy and riding him again, Kerry wanted a horse of her own. All the other kids on the Timber Ridge riding team had their own horses. It hadn't been so bad when Buccaneer was in the barn. But he'd just been taken down to his owner's farm in Pennsylvania, so Kerry didn't even have him to ride anymore.

Just then the front door banged shut. "Mom's home!" Holly yelled. She jumped off the bed, sending the magazines and newspapers scattering all over the floor. "Let's ask her where we can find you a horse for seven hundred dollars."

"You're still looking for that horse of yours, huh, Kerry?" Liz said with a smile as she dumped a couple of bags of groceries onto the kitchen table.

"Oh, Liz, it's awful," Kerry said. "We can't find *anything*."

Liz frowned. "I told you it wouldn't be easy, didn't I?"

"Mom, that's no help," Holly protested. "Can't you think of some place we can look?"

Liz shook her head. "Honestly, kids, I'm sorry. But unless someone's willing to lend Kerry a horse, I don't see how she's going to get what she wants."

"But Mom, she wants one of her own."

"I know she does. I wish I could help her out, but I can't."

Kerry knew Liz would lend her the extra money if she could afford it. But she also knew how expensive Holly's medical treatments had been. Liz was barely making ends meet as it was. There was no way she could afford to give Kerry money toward a horse.

"You could always ask 'Miss Super-Rich Whitney' to give you some of her extra money," Holly suggested in a nasty voice. "I bet she'd just love to help you out."

Kerry shot Holly an exasperated look. Whitney Myers was the *last* person who'd help her out!

"Speaking of Whitney," Liz said as she put the

6

groceries away, "I ran into Mrs. Myers in the village, and she told me that Whitney's cousin is coming to stay with them."

"Yuck!" Holly moaned. "I bet she's just as bad as Whitney."

Her mother smiled. "Well, you'll have plenty of time to find out. Angela's staying till next summer."

"Does she ride?" Kerry asked quietly, hoping Whitney's cousin didn't like horses. If that was the case, she probably wouldn't come to the barn much, and neither would Whitney.

"I haven't a clue," Liz said. "Mrs. Myers didn't say. All she said was that Angela would be here before the end of the summer." Then she took a letter out of her purse. "Oh, Kerry, I had a letter from your father today. You can stay with us for as long as you like. Holly and I love having you here."

Kerry suddenly felt embarrassed. She wanted to thank Liz for letting her stay with them, but she didn't know how. She took a deep breath. "I really love being here," she stammered out slowly. "And I—"

Liz cut her off. "I know what you're trying to say, Kerry," she said gently. "And you've no idea what you mean to Holly and me. You're part of our family."

"You bet she is," Holly agreed enthusiastically. "She's much better than a sister. And besides, with Whitney's cousin moving in, we've got to stick together!"

Kerry and Liz both laughed. But Kerry knew that Holly wasn't just kidding around. Whitney on her own was bad enough, but with a brand-new cousin to help her, there'd be no end to the things she could do to make Kerry's life miserable.

Chapter Two

Kerry breathed deeply, inhaling the sweet-smelling air. She loved riding the trails that bordered Timber Ridge. Everything was so green and fresh. Gently she squeezed Tally Ho with her legs and urged him closer to Magician. She'd never ridden Robin Lovell's horse before, but she was grateful that Robin had told her to ride him while she was away on vacation. If it hadn't been for Robin's generous offer, Kerry would have had to ride one of the small ponies that Liz used to teach the beginners.

As she came alongside Holly's black horse, Kerry remembered the first time she'd seen Holly. She had been swimming expertly around the Chapmans' pool but was totally unable to walk. Kerry glanced at Holly's legs. It was easy to forget that Holly had once been stuck in a wheelchair. From the way she rode her horse, it was impossible to tell that only months ago she'd been paralyzed.

"I wonder what Whitney's cousin is like?" Kerry mused as they rode along together.

Holly pulled an ugly face. "Yuck. I bet she's got tiny little squinty eyes, and a long nose, and huge teeth. Just like fangs."

Kerry burst out laughing. She'd been thinking almost the same thing ever since Liz had told them that Angela was coming to stay at Timber Ridge.

The trail got narrower, and the girls were forced to ride single file. Kerry eased back and let Holly take the lead. As they rode down the trail with its over-hanging cedars and pine trees, Kerry glanced up toward the mountain towering above them. She tried to imagine what it would feel like to be on skis, swooping down its winding ski trails.

"Hey, guess what?" Kerry said suddenly. She slowed her horse down and stared around her.

"What's the matter?"

"This is the trail I was on last week," Kerry said. "It leads to the other side of the mountain, and—"

Holly cut her off impatiently. "You mean we're near the place where you found Magician?"

"Yes."

"Let's go and see if that chestnut mare is still there."

Kerry urged Tally Ho into a trot and followed behind her friend, thinking about the series of events that had led her to the mare. Magician had escaped from his stall one night. After hours of searching, Kerry had found him on the other side of Timber Ridge Mountain, sharing a field with another horse that appeared to belong to a man who lived in an old shack. He had yelled at Kerry and tried to stop her when she'd taken Magician away. The mare had been in terrible shape, and Kerry had fantasized about rescuing the pathetic creature. But when she'd told Liz and Holly, they had both talked her out of it.

"Come on." Holly didn't wait for a reply. In a few seconds she was already way ahead of Kerry, riding up the wide ski trail toward the top of the hill.

"How far is it?" Holly yelled over her shoulder.

"About another ten minutes."

They rode to the top of the next hill. Suddenly the ground sloped down away from them, and Kerry saw the old shack in the distance. Smoke was curling lazily out of the old stone chimney, so she figured the owner was at home.

"Be quiet," Kerry warned as they approached the shack. It was just as dreadful as she remembered— leaning chimney, holes in the roof, and peeling paint. The front porch sagged at one end, and the steps leading up to it were rotted away.

Holly started to giggle nervously. Kerry held her breath, hoping the old man wouldn't come out and start yelling at them.

With Holly trying to stifle her muffled giggles, they rode past the house. No one came outside. Kerry heaved a sigh of relief. Up ahead, she could see the field where she'd found Magician. There in the far corner was the little shed that the horse lived in. Poor thing, she thought to herself. The mare had been thin, dirty, and horribly neglected. She couldn't understand why the awful old man owned a horse.

"Is that where you found Magician?" Holly asked in a loud stage whisper.

Kerry nodded and stood up in her stirrups, hoping to catch a glimpse of the chestnut horse.

The field was empty.

"Maybe she's inside the shed," Holly suggested hopefully.

Magician whinnied, as if he remembered his recent pasture mate. But there was no sign of the chestnut mare.

"I'll go and look for her." Kerry dismounted and handed Tally Ho's reins to Holly. Crouching down, she slipped under the fence and started walking across the field. She wished she'd brought some carrots with her. That chestnut mare had looked half starved, and there was hardly any grass in the field. It was full of weeds and rocks.

She ran up to the shed and looked inside, expecting to find the horse. But the shed was empty, except for a few piles of dried-up manure and some old bread crusts that were lying in the dirt with hordes of flies buzzing around them. She stepped outside and looked around the field again. It wasn't very big; there was nowhere the horse could be hiding.

"She's not in there!" Kerry cried as she ran back toward Holly.

"Are you sure?"

"Of course I am." Kerry slipped back under the fence, took her horse's reins, and vaulted nimbly onto the saddle. "She's gone."

"I wonder what he did with her?" Holly mused thoughtfully as she stared at the old man's tumbledown shack.

For an awful moment Kerry remembered what

Holly had said when she'd told her about the old man and his horse. Holly had made a dreadful joke about him owning a horse so he could eat it. She shivered slightly. Holly's joke didn't seem quite so funny now.

Just then they heard an angry shout, and Kerry's stomach did several violent flip-flops. "Let's get out of here," she said urgently as she dug her heels into Tally Ho's sides. The old man was standing on his porch, shaking his fist at them. Unfortunately, to get back to Timber Ridge they had to ride within fifteen feet of where he stood.

"You get off my property!" he screamed in a high-pitched voice as they rode down the trail.

Kerry tried to stop herself, but it was too late. The words were out of her mouth before she had a chance to think. "What did you do with your horse?"

Holly gasped and skidded Magician to a stop in front of her. "Come on," she hissed through her teeth. "Don't stop and talk to him."

"I want to find out about that horse," Kerry replied under her breath. She turned and stared at the old man. He was wearing the same filthy sweatpants and sweatshirt that he'd worn the last time she'd seen him, and he still hadn't shaved.

"Where's your horse?" she insisted, her heart pounding.

"What's it to you?" he yelled back. Then he lurched down the rickety-looking steps and stopped about ten feet away.

Kerry wanted to run away, but all she could think about was the little chestnut mare with its tangled mane and large, sad brown eyes. She swallowed her

12

fear and ignored Holly's urgent suggestion that they leave as fast as they could. "What have you done with her?" she asked again.

"Sold her." The old man swayed from side to side, then took two steps toward them.

"Who did you sell her to?"

"None of your business. Now, get off my property!" And with an angry snort, he staggered across his front yard.

"Kerry!" Holly screamed.

She needed no urging. In a flash she kicked Tally Ho as hard as she could, and the horse bolted forward into a fast trot. The old man tried to grab at the horse's reins, but the fence got in his way. He staggered against it and fell over, cursing loudly.

With her heart almost jumping out of her mouth, Kerry followed Holly and Magician up the hill. Tally Ho was cantering now. Even though they were putting a healthy distance between the old man and themselves, she could still hear him shouting and swearing at them.

"Phew," Holly said finally when the shack was no longer in sight. "That was a close one. Why did you have to stop and talk to him?"

"Because I wanted to find out what he'd done with his horse."

"Too late now," Holly muttered. "She's gone, and I don't want to go back and ask him where she is."

Liz was waiting for them when they got back to the barn an hour later. "Hurry up and put your horses away," she said with a smile. "I think I might have an idea about a horse for Kerry."

"What is it, Mom?" Holly asked eagerly.

"I'll tell you when you're finished with the horses."

As Kerry expertly ran a brush over Tally Ho's back, she wondered what Liz had come up with. Maybe she'd seen a "horse for sale" advertisement that they'd missed, or perhaps knew of someone selling a horse that would be perfect for her. She was getting excited.

As soon as she had finished, she ran into Liz's office. Holly was already there, sitting on an old tack trunk.

"Look at this," Liz said, and she handed them the latest issue of the local newspaper.

"What? I don't see anything, Mom."

"Down there, at the bottom of the page."

"'Jackson's Consignment Sale,'" Holly read out slowly. Then she frowned. "Mom, what does *consignment* mean?"

"Read a bit farther."

"It's a horse auction!" Kerry cried out suddenly, pulling the newspaper out of Holly's hands.

Liz smiled. "That's right. And it might be the answer, Kerry. If you know what you're doing, you can sometimes get a really good horse at an auction without spending a small fortune."

"Mom, can we go?" Holly asked, her eyes shining with excitement.

"Yes, of course we can. It's on Saturday night, and if you like, we'll have dinner out first, and then go to the auction."

"Will they be selling anything besides horses?" Kerry asked. This was *really* exciting. She'd never been to an auction before.

"Oh, yes. I expect they'll have used saddles and bridles, and horse blankets, and all sorts of stuff. I need some extra blankets for the winter, and I know we could use more buckets. I hope to get everything I need while I'm there." Then she paused and frowned. "Kerry," she said slowly, "you haven't told me how your father's going to feel about you buying a horse. Have you told him yet?"

Kerry hesitated before answering, knowing she'd have to bluff her way out of it. "He won't mind," she replied quietly. "He loves horses."

"Kerry," Liz said gently, "loving horses and actually owning one are two very different things. I think you'd better write and tell him what you're planning to do."

"Okay," Kerry muttered, and crossed her fingers. Actually, she had no idea how her father would react to the news. With his constant traveling, having a horse in the family might not exactly fit in with his future plans. She'd worry about it after the auction, Kerry decided, and pushed all thoughts of her father out of her mind. Instead, she dreamed about going to the auction and finding the perfect horse. In her imagination it was a beautiful light bay with a small white star in the middle of its forehead. Or perhaps a golden chestnut with a silvery-colored mane and tail, like the horse in one of her favorite stories.

Chapter Three

Kerry was so excited she could hardly eat her dinner, even though it was one of her favorites—sausage pizza with extra cheese. All she could think about was the horse she was going to buy at the auction.

As they ate their meal, Liz explained to the two girls what a consignment sale and auction was like. "All the horses there will have a price listed in the sale catalog," she said. "Their owners will have put down the lowest price that they're willing to accept. Then it's up to the auctioneer to get the bidding up as high as he can. You see, he gets a percentage of the final selling price, so it's in his best interests to get the highest possible price."

"Do they have horses for seven hundred dollars?" Holly asked through a mouthful of hot pizza.

"Sometimes. And we'd better get there early so we'll have time to check the horses over carefully before they go into the selling ring."

Kerry waited impatiently for Liz to finish her coffee. She pushed her plate of half-eaten pizza away from her and glanced at her watch. In another couple of hours she might be the proud owner of a brand-new horse. Then she looked in her purse. The twenty-five dollars was still safely tucked away at the bottom. Liz had told her not to bring the whole seven hundred with her in case it got lost or stolen. If they did find a horse for her to buy, Liz was going to write a check, and Kerry would pay her back. But she'd taken the twenty-five out of her savings account because she wanted to buy her horse a new halter, and maybe some grooming brushes so she wouldn't have to borrow Holly's stuff all the time.

Finally Liz finished her coffee and paid the bill. The auction barn was only a ten-minute drive from the center of Winchester. As they approached it, Kerry's excitement rose.

Jackson's Auction was held in a collection of old barn buildings, and already there were crowds of people there. "Where are all the horses?" Kerry asked anxiously. All she could see were long tables, piled high with every kind of horse equipment imaginable. Liz wasn't going to have any trouble finding what she wanted. Kerry only hoped that the selection of horses would be as large and varied as the tack and equipment.

"Why don't you read this?" Liz handed each girl a brochure. "It lists all the horses with a brief description of each one, and also the minimum price set by the owner."

Kerry's hopes fell as she quickly read the listings. Of the ten horses offered for sale that evening, only two of them had starting prices that she could afford.

"Kerry, the brown gelding sounds pretty good," Holly said thoughtfully. "He's number eight." Holly reached over and pointed to the listing in Kerry's brochure.

She nodded slowly and read number eight's description to herself. "Dark brown gelding, nine years old, sixteen hands, good hunter prospect. Sound, no vices. Starting price: five hundred dollars."

"Maybe no one else will want him," Holly said hopefully.

Kerry read the only other possibility. "Number three, gray mare, seven years old, good intermediate horse. Low bid: seven hundred dollars."

"Let's go and look at them." Holly took her arm and dragged her over to the line of horse stalls in the back of the main barn. Each stall had a number tacked over it, corresponding to the catalog listing of the horse.

Kerry looked enviously at the big, dark bay horse in the first stall. She'd read his description in her brochure and wished she could afford to buy him. He was only five years old, and he reminded her of Buccaneer. But his owners wouldn't accept less than nine hundred dollars for him, so Kerry sadly, but firmly, put him out of her mind.

Then she looked at number three, the gray mare, and decided she wasn't a bad-looking horse. But there were several other interested buyers outside its stall. Kerry had the feeling that the horse would sell for more than its seven-hundred-dollar list price.

That left number eight. The brown gelding was a solid, stocky-looking horse with a very short tail and enormous hindquarters. And when he turned around to look at her, Kerry winced. He had a huge white blaze that practically covered his whole face, and one of his eyes was brown while the other one was a bright blue.

"Yuck! He looks just like a cow!" Holly exclaimed. "Give him a pair of horns, and you'd never know the difference."

Kerry miserably agreed with her. Number eight was definitely an ugly horse. But if he was all she could afford, even an ugly horse with mismatched eyes that looked like a cow was better than no horse at all.

Just then Kerry noticed a small doorway at the end of the row of stalls. "I wonder what's in there," she said to Holly.

"Oh, you don't want to go in there, miss," said a man's voice right behind her.

Kerry turned around quickly. A man in a red-checkered shirt was looking at her with a friendly smile. "Why not?" she asked curiously.

"That's where they keep the 'other' horses."

"What *other* horses?" Holly asked. She stared toward the doorway. It was pretty dark beyond, and she was intrigued.

The man's smile faded. "They always sell off a few reject horses at these sales, but they're really in bad shape. Most of them end up at the dog food factory. Don't go and look at them, miss. It'll only upset you. It even bothers me."

Kerry was just about to ignore his warning when Liz hurried up to them with an armful of stuff she'd bought at the sale. "I need your help," she said. "I want to get all this out to the car before the auction starts. I can't carry all of it by myself."

Holly giggled and asked her mother if she'd left anything behind for anyone else to buy. Liz had obviously been very successful. It took them two trips to the car to load it up with the winter horse blankets, feed buckets, and other supplies that Liz had bought for the stables.

By the time they had finished, the horse auction was just beginning, and Kerry had no chance to go and look at the reject horses that the man in the red-checkered shirt had mentioned.

The dark bay gelding finally sold for fifteen hundred dollars, and Kerry couldn't help feeling envious as its delighted new owner led him out of the ring. He was a beautiful horse. She wished she could have bid on him. The next horse, a buckskin two-year-old, went for eleven hundred dollars, and Kerry started to get anxious. Her precious seven hundred was beginning to look awfully small compared to what most of the horses were selling for.

"Here she is," Holly whispered as number three, the gray mare was led into the small auction ring.

Kerry studied her critically. Liz told her in a low voice that she had also checked her over in her stall and thought she was a good horse. For a few minutes the auctioneer, a large fat man in a bright yellow shirt, couldn't seem to get anyone in the audience to bid on the gray mare.

"Hold your arm up, Kerry," Liz advised.

"Will I get her for seven hundred?" Kerry asked, knowing it was the lowest price the owners would accept.

"Yes, as long as no one else bids any higher."

Kerry started to get excited. She really liked the pretty gray mare. So she quickly raised her right arm.

The auctioneer's wary eyes spotted her immediately, and he announced loudly he had an opening bid of seven hundred dollars. There was a muffled noise from the audience, but no one else offered a higher bid. Kerry crossed her fingers and held her breath.

"Going once," the auctioneer barked out loudly.

"Going twice," he continued after a short pause. He looked toward the audience hopefully.

"She's yours," Holly squealed with anticipation.

"Seven hundred and *fifty* dollars!"

Kerry's heart almost stopped beating. She looked around wildly to see who'd just spoken. But before she could see who it was, another voice called, "Eight hundred."

The gray mare finally sold for twelve hundred dollars, but not to Kerry.

"Rotten luck," Holly muttered sympathetically as the gray mare left the ring. "I guess the 'cow' is your only hope."

Kerry grimaced and wished the brown gelding wasn't such an ugly horse. Of course, no one was forcing her to buy him, but she was getting desperate. She wanted a horse of her own, and she needed

it in time for the Timber Ridge riding team's next event. The Winchester Charity Horse Show was at the end of the summer, and Kerry was determined to be in it, riding her own horse and beating Whitney Myers as well!

It took another half hour before it was number eight's turn to be sold. A wave of laughter rippled through the audience when the brown gelding was led into the ring. "He oughta be in a cattle auction!" a loud voice rang out, and everyone laughed.

The horse was big and solid. Kerry felt sorry for him as he was led around the ring while the audience joked about the way he looked.

"Do you want *that* one?" Liz asked.

"It's the only one left," Kerry muttered miserably, still staring at the horse's cowlike face.

"You don't have to buy him," Liz said. "There'll probably be another horse auction next month. Why don't you wait till then?"

Kerry didn't want to wait. If the ugly brown horse was all she could afford, then she'd buy him. She knew she could learn to love him . . . eventually.

To everyone's surprise, a bid of five hundred and fifty dollars was called out. Kerry raised her hand.

"Six hundred," the auctioneer boomed out, smiling at her. Then he looked around the audience hopefully.

"Six fifty!" a voice yelled from the back of the audience.

Kerry turned around. It was the man in the red-checkered shirt. She hoped he wouldn't want to go any higher. She raised her hand again. "Seven hundred dollars," she said in a loud, clear voice.

There was a brief silence.

"Do I hear any more bids?" The auctioneer smiled at Kerry again.

"Seven fifty!" the man's voice yelled into the silence.

"I'll lend you a hundred dollars if you *really* want him," Liz offered quickly.

Kerry was tempted. But as she looked again at the homely horse, she couldn't go through with it. He'd always be an ugly horse, and she'd probably end up hating him. Sadly she shook her head and thanked Liz for the offer of help.

The brown gelding was sold to the man in the red-checkered shirt for seven hundred and fifty dollars.

"Well, I guess this is it, then," Liz said with a yawn.

"Mom, I want to watch the rest of the horses being sold," Holly said in a pleading voice.

Her mother hesitated, then smiled. "Okay, but I'm exhausted. I'll wait for you kids in the car."

Liz walked off through the crowd as the next horse was brought into the ring. It was a flashy black and white pinto, and it eventually sold for eighteen hundred dollars. The last horse went for even more. Kerry had the awful feeling that she was never going to find the horse of her dreams at an auction, or anywhere else. Her perfect horse existed only in her imagination.

After the last horse had been sold, Holly wandered off to look at a rack of used saddles and bridles. Kerry remained where she was while the crowds around her slowly dispersed. The auctioneer disappeared toward the back of the barn, and all of a sudden Kerry remembered what the man in the red-checkered shirt had said about the reject horses.

Making sure Holly was still occupied with the used saddles, Kerry slipped away quietly and approached the doorway. All the horse stalls were empty, and she felt a surge of envy for the ten happy new horse owners.

She hesitated at the open door, then slowly peered around the corner. Several people were in the small barn, including the auctioneer. There wasn't much light, but she could see his bright yellow shirt clearly. He seemed to be arguing with someone. Every now and then he waved his arms. She edged a little closer, not too sure she was even supposed to be in this barn.

"It's worth at least fifty, and you know it, Tom Burton," the auctioneer's voice rang out loudly.

Kerry shrank back against the wall and hid herself in the shadows behind a bulkhead. Three people, including the auctioneer, were standing together at the far end of the barn. One of them was holding on to a horse. Kerry blinked her eyes and tried to see what the animal looked like, but it was too dark. The only light in the barn came from a weak light bulb hanging amid a shroud of cobwebs high in the rafters over her head.

"You're a *thief*!" another voice exclaimed angrily. "I'll give you thirty-five, and not a penny more."

"Done!" The auctioneer laughed and clapped the other man loudly on his back. Then he held out his hand, and Kerry guessed that another horse had been sold. Probably one of the rejects that never came out of the back barn and into the selling ring.

The auctioneer didn't see her as he and another man strode past her on their way back toward the main barn. She crouched down low behind the bulkhead, wondering where the third man was. The one who'd just paid thirty-five dollars for a horse.

A feeling of nausea arose inside her as she realized what the thirty-five-dollar horse's fate was going to be. She shook her head, trying to banish the vision of cans of dog food, all lined up neatly on supermarket shelves.

Just as she was about to slip back inside the bigger barn, she heard a soft whinny, then a harsh male voice: "Come on, I haven't got all night!"

Kerry couldn't move. The pitiful whinney had reminded her of something. Then the odd pieces of the jigsaw puzzle started to fall into place. It all fitted together, but she had to make sure.

Summoning all of her courage, she crept out of her hiding place and slowly walked toward the far end of the barn. There was a large open doorway, and through it she could see the moon shining brightly behind a grove of trees outside. There was no sign of the man and his thirty-five-dollar horse, but Kerry knew he couldn't have gone far. She was bursting with curiosity. She had to see for herself if her suspicions were correct.

Chapter Four

The moon was very bright, and it cast long, sinister shadows across the open parking lot behind the barn. Kerry dodged out of the way of a departing car as she looked around at the odd assortment of horse vans and trailers that were starting to leave.

She paused for a moment, hoping she wouldn't pick the wrong one. Turning away from a flashy red and gold four-horse van, she suddenly spotted an ancient cattle trailer behind a gray pickup truck. That's probably it, she thought as she quickly ran toward it.

Her heart almost jumped out of her mouth when someone suddenly grabbed her arm.

"Kerry, I've been looking for you *everywhere*!"

"Phew." Kerry exhaled slowly, her heart still thumping loudly. "You scared me to death, Holly."

"Mom's waiting for us. Come on."

Kerry shook herself free of Holly's hand. "Give me a second," she said impatiently. The pickup truck's

28

engine had just roared into life. There wasn't much time.

"Where are you going?" Holly cried as Kerry ran toward the truck.

Kerry ignored her. The truck with the cattle trailer was slowly backing away from the fence. She jumped up as high as she could, but she couldn't see what was inside it. She ran toward the front of the truck. "Excuse me, but would you mind stopping for a moment?"

The man behind the wheel looked at her in astonishment, and Kerry had to force herself not to run away. He had a dark, narrow face, and his eyes were almost black and set very close together.

"What do you want?" he hissed.

"Did you just buy a horse?"

He glared at her angrily. "None of your business. Now, get out of my way, or I'll run you over."

Kerry stepped back. "Please," she stammered as the truck started to move again. "Please stop and let me see it."

The man hesitated, then slammed his brakes on. The truck lurched forward, then shuddered to a halt. "Why do you want to see my horse?" he growled.

"Because I think your horse belonged to a . . . to someone I know," Kerry finished lamely, hoping he'd believe her lie.

The man sneered at her. "I doubt it, unless you hang out with the town drunk!"

Kerry tried to keep her nerves under control. Now she was sure she was right. "Please," she begged one more time.

"Oh, all right, but hurry up," the man grumbled under his breath as he opened the door and got out of his truck.

Holly ran up just as he was unfastening the bolts on the back ramp of the cattle trailer. "Have you gone nuts, Kerry Logan?" she hissed loudly.

"Okay," the man said nastily as he lowered the ramp. "Now are you satisfied?"

Kerry pushed past him and walked up the short, steep ramp and into the trailer. "It *is* her," she said softly as she stared at the frightened horse that was trying desperately to back away.

"*Who?*" Holly demanded loudly.

"The old man's chestnut mare. I've found her."

"Have you two finished gawking at my horse?" the man asked impatiently.

"I've got to buy her," Kerry whispered urgently.

Holly stared first at the neglected horse, then at her friend's determined expression. "But *why?* She looks ten times worse than the cow-faced one."

"Because if I don't, she'll end up in a can of dog food."

Holly's face turned as white as a sheet. "You're kidding."

"No, I'm not. Now, look, I've only got twenty-five in my purse, and I don't think this man will take a check. Go and ask Liz for all the spare cash she has, and hurry. *Please.*"

Holly opened her mouth as if she was going to argue. But another look at Kerry's grim face changed her mind. "All right." Then she scurried off to find her mother.

"I'll give you forty dollars for her," Kerry said as calmly as she could. The chestnut mare whinnied softly and tried to pull herself loose from the chains that tied her halter to the side of the trailer.

"Nuthin' doing," the man growled in a low voice. "I just paid a hundred dollars for her—"

Kerry cut him off angrily. "No, you didn't. I was there, and you only paid thirty-five!"

"You little sneak." The man glared at her, his narrow eyes looking even blacker than before.

"Forty dollars." Kerry wished she felt as confident as she sounded. Inside, her stomach was heaving, and her legs felt like gelatin. She looked around anxiously for Holly and Liz.

"Seventy-five," the man suddenly snapped. He put his hand on the horse's thin rump. The mare quivered and tried again to pull loose from her chains.

"Forty-five," Kerry offered immediately, hoping Liz would have enough extra cash to cover the difference.

Just then Holly returned. "Mom's on her way," she said breathlessly.

"You're wasting my time," the man grunted loudly. He grabbed Kerry's arm and began to pull her out of the trailer.

"Take your hands off her, Tom Burton!" Liz's voice rang out sternly, and Kerry heaved a sigh of relief. Help had arrived!

Holly gasped loudly. "Mom, do you *know* him?"

Liz stared at the man angrily. "Everyone knows Tom Burton," she said in a dangerously controlled voice. "I see you're up to your old tricks again, Tom."

"Mom, what are you talking about?"

"Shhh, Holly. Stay out of this."

Kerry leaned gratefully against the side of the metal trailer and listened to Liz tell Tom Burton exactly what she thought of him. She accused him of sneaking around at horse auctions and buying horses that no one else wanted so he could sell them illegally to the dog food manufacturers.

"Someone's got to do it," he muttered.

"Yes, but they've got *licenses*, and you don't, do you?" Liz challenged him.

He stared at her without saying a word.

"How much did you pay for this mare?" Liz asked.

"Thirty-five dollars," Kerry blurted out. Tom Burton shot her a murderous look.

"And how much could you have *sold* her for?"

He hesitated, his dark eyes gleaming greedily in the gloom of the trailer. "At least a hundred," he finally said in a whining voice.

"Horse feathers!" Liz snapped. Then she fumbled around in her purse and pulled out a handful of money. She hesitated and looked anxiously toward Kerry. "Are you really sure you want to go through with this?"

Kerry glanced at the poor little chestnut mare. Her coat was caked with mud, and her mane was just as knotted and tangled with twigs and leaves as it had been when she'd first seen her in the old man's field. Of course no one would bother to clean her up if he were only going to sell her for dog food. She gulped and nodded her head. "Yes," she said firmly. It was the only thing she *could* do she knew she'd never forgive herself if she let Tom Burton take the mare away

and sell her to the meat market.

"I'll take sixty dollars and not a penny less," Tom Burton said.

"Forty-five, and *I* won't tell the police about your illegal horse-selling business," Liz snapped back.

The man hesitated for a second or two, then shrugged his shoulders helplessly. "You win," he said between clenched teeth as he fumbled around, undoing the horse's chains.

"Mom, you *did* it," Holly squealed with delight.

"And heaven only knows why," Liz murmured thoughtfully as Tom Burton backed the scruffy chestnut horse down the ramp. She ran her experienced eyes quickly over the pathetic little horse and put her arm around Kerry's shoulders. "This one's a real charity case," she said gently. "The best thing we can do for her is feed her some good food, clean her up, and then sell her off to someone who just wants a big pet. She'll never amount to more than that, I'm afraid."

"She's awfully thin," Holly remarked as they were leading the mare toward their own horse trailer.

"All she needs is lots of love," Kerry said. She didn't want to argue with Liz's idea about getting the horse better and then selling it; she was just grateful that Liz hadn't stopped her from rescuing the mare.

The mare balked at the sight of the open trailer. She stopped suddenly and tried to pull away from Kerry. "Don't be scared," Kerry whispered softly. "I won't hurt you."

"This poor animal's had some rough treatment," Liz said sympathetically as she gently put her arm behind the mare's rump and pushed her forward.

The mare squealed and scrambled up the ramp and into the trailer. Once inside, Kerry was able to examine her more closely. In the bright light of the trailer, she looked worse than before! Her mane, all tangled up with bits of twigs and dirt, looked gray and dingy. Kerry wet her hand in the water bucket and gently rubbed at a hunk of mane. Then she looked closer. Some of the dirt had washed away, and the mare's mane wasn't a dingy gray after all. It was a silvery flaxen color!

Startled by her discovery, Kerry began to pick away at a clump of mud and dead hair on the mare's neck. She wet her hand again and saw that the horse's coat was really a rich, golden chestnut brown.

"Golden chestnut, with a silvery mane and tail."

The words ran through her mind, and she suddenly realized that this run-down horse just might be the horse she'd always dreamed about.

Reluctantly she left her new horse in the trailer and went to join Liz and Holly in the car. They were still talking about what Kerry could do to fix the horse up so she could sell it.

As Kerry listened to them, she knew they were wrong. Deep down inside, Kerry knew that the chestnut mare was the horse she'd always dreamed about, and she was determined to keep her. She'd work harder than ever before. And at the end of the summer she *and* her new horse were going to surprise everyone.

They were going to enter the Winchester Charity Horse Show and win!

Chapter Five

Magician whinnied loudly when he saw the chestnut mare. "He remembers her!" Holly exclaimed. She left Kerry holding her new horse and ran toward Magician's stall.

"Where should I put her, Liz?" Kerry asked. She glanced nervously at her new purchase, comparing her neglected appearance to the sleek horses in the barn.

"In the empty stall next to Magician." Liz walked down the aisle with an armful of hay. "Don't feed her any grain till we've had the vet check her out," she warned. "This poor little horse is half starved, and we don't want her to colic."

Kerry noticed immediately that her mare calmed down as soon as Magician stuck his black, velvety muzzle over the stall partition.

"I think he's in love with her," Holly chortled. She stuck her head around the door. "How's she doing?"

"Better now that Magician's here," Kerry replied. She smiled at the new mare. The horse had stopped trembling and was eagerly rubbing noses with Magician.

"He's probably telling her what a great place this is," Holly joked.

Kerry grinned and headed for the tackroom. She was itching to get some of the dirt out of the mare's coat.

"Hey, Kerry! It's almost midnight!" Liz exclaimed. "Don't start grooming her now."

"But, Liz—"

"Bedtime," Liz replied firmly. "You can brush her all day tomorrow. Besides, she needs time to settle in and adjust to her new surroundings before you two get going on her."

Kerry reluctantly tore herself away from the mare, but she was confident that the horse would settle in as long as she had Magician beside her. It was obvious they'd formed a strong attachment to one another during their brief acquaintance in the old man's field.

"Have you thought of a name for her yet?" Holly asked as they walked back to the house.

Kerry shook her head. She was too excited to think clearly about a name for her new horse. "No," she said. "Got any ideas?"

"Uh—uh. I'm too tired. I'll think of something in the morning."

When Kerry awoke the next morning and looked at her alarm clock, she groaned loudly. It was almost ten-thirty, and she'd overslept. She jumped out of bed and ran into Holly's room. "Come on, wake up!" she cried. "We've got to go to the barn."

Holly opened one eye and wrinkled her nose. "Go away," she muttered sleepily. "I wanna sleep."

"You can't." Kerry pulled all the bedclothes onto the floor with a dramatic flourish. "I'll fix you a bowl of cereal," she said, hoping to bribe her out of her bed with the offer of breakfast.

"Big deal," Holly replied with a yawn. "I want pancakes and sausage!"

Kerry snorted impatiently and disappeared back into her own room to get dressed. She quickly pulled on a pair of jeans and a pale green sweatshirt. Then she decided to skip breakfast altogether. She was much too eager to see how her new horse had survived its first night in the barn.

Liz was already in the outside riding ring with a group of beginning students by the time Holly and Kerry got to the barn.

"I've called the vet!" Liz yelled out as the girls walked by. "He's coming over tomorrow to check your horse out, Kerry."

"She's okay, isn't she?" Kerry yelled back anxiously.

"She's fine. We'll talk about it later, okay?"

Kerry hoped the barn's veterinarian wouldn't find anything wrong with her new horse. Liz had told her it would be wise to have Doctor Kruger check her out thoroughly, and also have the barn's farrier trim her hooves. They were much too long and were also full of cracks and chips.

She ran the last few steps toward the barn eagerly, then stopped suddenly. Holly, who was right behind her, did her best to avoid a collision.

"What did you stop for?" Holly yelped as she tried to keep herself from falling over.

"Oh, no!" Kerry wailed, looking straight ahead of her down the aisle toward the horse stalls.

Holly peered over her shoulder. "Just ignore her," she whispered loudly.

"How? She's right outside Magician's stall. And I bet that's her cousin." Kerry clenched and unclenched her fists. Why did Whitney Myers's cousin have to arrive at Timber Ridge today, of all days?

Trying to remain as nonchalant as possible, Kerry walked up the aisle. It wasn't easy pretending to be perfectly calm, because all she really wanted to do was stare at Whitney's cousin. Angela Pearson was like a reverse image of Whitney. She had light blond hair, whereas Whitney's was almost black, and a deeply tanned complexion in contrast to Whitney's pale, creamy one. But as Kerry drew closer, she could see that the cousins' startling differences were made even more dramatic by their eyes. Angela's eyes were exactly like Whitney's—pale, pale blue. And right now, both pairs of them were staring right at her.

"I didn't know we were running a halfway house for derelict horses," Whitney said with a scornful laugh. Then she waved toward the chestnut mare's stall. "This is *really* embarrassing. I was just telling Angela what great horses we had at the barn. Then I find this disgusting bag of bones in here."

"Yeah," Angela agreed. She glanced toward Astronaut's stall, where the handsome bay horse stood looking at them through the bars. "He's a beautiful

horse. Not a bit like this one!" She tossed her pale blond hair away from her face and grinned at her cousin.

"She's Kerry's new horse," Holly blurted out angrily. "So you can just stop being rude about her."

"Hah! She looks like she ought to go to the dog food factory," Whitney snapped sarcastically.

"She almost did. Kerry rescued her last night."

"What a shame. Now Rover won't get his dinner!"

Angela exploded with laughter. "Not even a cat could get a decent meal off that horse!"

Kerry knew that her worst fears about Whitney's cousin had come true. From the way the new girl was smiling and enjoying Whitney's nasty comments, Kerry sensed she was just like her cousin: mean, rotten, and selfish.

"Just you wait, Holly Chapman," Whitney threatened. "My mother won't stand for this—this fleabag. I'll get her to call Liz right away. We don't allow horses like this to live at Timber Ridge." Then she stopped and glared at Kerry. "Trust you to do something really dumb like this. Thank goodness you won't be here forever. I can't wait till your father gets back and takes you away. Then things can get back to normal around here."

Holly smiled sweetly and looked directly at Angela Pearson. "By that she means she can start cheating her way back into the blue ribbons," she said in an innocent voice.

Whitney's pale blue eyes narrowed dangerously, but she turned away from Kerry and Holly. With a toss of her dark shoulder-length hair, she said, "Come on,

Angela. Let's go and tell my mother about the latest 'horse' in the barn."

"Don't worry about *her*," Holly said reassuringly as Whitney and Angela stalked out of the barn. "Mrs. Myers can't force you to get rid of your horse."

Kerry wasn't so sure. Whitney's mother was president of the Timber Ridge Homeowners' Association, which owned and controlled the stables. She knew Whitney would never give up trying to force her to leave Timber Ridge.

She pushed Whitney's threats out of her mind as she approached the stall next to Magician's. Gently Kerry opened the door. The frightened mare backed away from her at once. "Come on, girl," she said softly, easing into the stall and holding out her hand. The mare's nose twitched, but she looked at the carrot that Kerry was offering. And after a moment's hesitation, she greedily snatched it from her outstretched hand.

"What are you going to do with her first?" Holly asked from the open doorway.

"Give her a bath. If she'll let me."

"Want some help?" Holly offered with a grin.

Moments later, armed with buckets, sponges, and the barn's hosepipe, the two girls led the chestnut mare outside and tied her up underneath a large maple tree. Kerry watched concerned as the horse kept neighing loudly.

"Maybe she'll settle down if Magician's next to her," Holly suggested. "I'll go get him."

Once Magician was beside her, the chestnut mare quieted down, and Kerry started working shampoo into her filthy coat. Besides all the mud that was caked in it, there was still a lot of old dead hair left over from the previous winter. As it started to wash away, Kerry was overjoyed to see that she hadn't been mistaken the night before. The horse's coat was turning out to be a rich, golden chestnut color that would become even richer as the mare got healthier.

While Holly worked at getting the tangles and dirt out of the horse's tail, Kerry turned her attention to its mane. Patiently she unsnarled the knots and twigs. When she'd finished, she washed it thoroughly. All her hard work paid off. By the time she rinsed all the soap out, she could see that the mare's mane was an exquisite shade of pale, silvery gold.

"She looks great!" Holly cried enthusiastically when they had finally finished.

Kerry smiled happily. Already the hot sun was drying off the horse's coat. As long as she ignored the mare's visible ribs and prominent withers, she really didn't look too bad. Now all she had to do was fatten her up and get her strong again.

"Good grief!" Liz exclaimed loudly when she saw the transformation that had taken place. "She's really quite beautiful, Kerry. Are you sure this is the same horse we brought home last night?"

"Do you *really* like her?" Kerry asked, feeling nervous and proud at the same time.

Liz nodded her head approvingly as she walked around the mare. She ran her expert hands down the horse's fine-boned legs, examined her eyes closely, and then opened her mouth and looked at her teeth. "Not much more than five years old, I'd say," Liz muttered when she'd finished her critical inspection. "And from the way she looks right now, I'd even be willing to bet she's got some good breeding in her. But that'll be easier to tell after we get some meat on her bones."

Kerry was delighted with Liz's approval. She'd done the right thing when she'd rescued her little chestnut mare.

While Liz and Kerry admired the newly washed horse, Holly went into the barn and got the measuring stick. Liz gently placed the horizontal bar on the highest point of the mare's bony withers and declared in a surprised voice, "Look! She's almost fifteen and a half hands. I didn't realize she was this big."

"We'll have to stop calling her the 'little' chestnut mare," Holly said as she pulled the measuring stick away from the horse's shoulder.

"Kerry, what *are* you going to call her?" Liz asked.

Kerry frowned. "I don't know, Liz," she said slowly, staring at her new horse. "I can't seem to think of anything."

"What do *you* think, Mom?" Holly asked.

Liz tilted her head to one side and stared at Kerry's new horse thoughtfully. "You know," she said slowly, "this reminds me of the time, years ago, when my mother bought a filthy pillow at a tag sale. We all told her she was crazy, but she ignored us, thank goodness. Because after she'd had the pillow cleaned, it turned out to be an exquisite piece of needlepoint. It was really very beautiful."

"Just like Kerry's horse!" Holly said.

"Exactly. And maybe there's the right name for her hidden in my story," Liz said.

"We could call her Pillow," Holly suggested with a grin. "Or how about Needlepoint?"

Kerry pulled a disgusted face and threatened to squirt her friend with the hosepipe. "What's another name like needlepoint, Liz?" she asked after Holly had pulled the hosepipe out of her hands.

"Hmmm, let me think." Liz paused for a moment. "Well, there's embroidery, and bargello, and of course crewel work."

Holly, never the one to miss an opportunity to make a pun, said, "Let's call her Crewel. After all, someone was very *cruel* to let her get into this rotten condition!"

Kerry threw up her hands in despair and went for the hosepipe again. Holly really deserved to be squirted for that one!

"No, wait! I think I've got it," Liz said suddenly. And then she smiled. "How about Tapestry as a name for your horse?"

"Liz, that's perfect. I *love* it!" Kerry cried at once, and she flung her arms around her horse's still-damp neck and hugged her.

"Mom, what is a tapestry?"

"It's a beautiful old wall hanging, Holly. You usually find them in museums, or churches. Long, long ago, people used to embroider scenes of their lives on large pieces of cloth. The most famous tapestry of all is called the *Bayeux* tapestry. It's almost a thousand years old, and it's hanging in a palace in Normandy, France."

45

"Wow," Holly said in awe.

"Come on Tapestry," Kerry said, liking the sound of her horse's new name. "Let's go and meet everyone." She'd just noticed Sue Armstrong and Jennifer McKenna leading their horses out of the barn. They looked as if they were getting ready to go trail riding.

"She's very pretty," Jennifer said with a smile, "but isn't she awfully thin?"

"Have you ridden her yet?" Sue asked as she settled herself comfortably in Tara's saddle. Then she stared closely at Kerry's new horse. "Looks like she needs some fattening up."

Kerry grinned happily, refusing to be dismayed by her friends' lack of enthusiasm over the new horse. She knew everything was going to work out all right.

As the two girls on horseback rode out of the stable yard toward the woods and trails, Sue's question echoed in her mind. Kerry realized in a panic that she had absolutely no idea whether Tapestry was even broken to the saddle! Suppose she'd never had anyone on her back before. Kerry hadn't even considered that important little detail!

Her secret plans for being a part of the Timber Ridge riding team at the Winchester Charity Horse Show began to fade. If Tapestry had never been ridden before, she'd never be in the horse show.

But she *had* to! The one thing Kerry wanted more than anything was to beat Whitney Myers and silence her spiteful tongue forever. After the horrible things Whitney had said about Tapestry that morning, Kerry wouldn't be satisfied until she'd won the blue ribbon in the jumping class—riding her very own horse.

Chapter Six

"The first thing you've got to do," Liz said early the next morning, "is to get Tapestry to trust you."

Kerry ran the brush carefully down the mare's shoulder and turned around.

"And lots of grooming, too," Liz continued. "She's been starved of more than food. She needs lots of company, especially yours."

"Maybe Kerry ought to sleep in the barn with her," Holly suggested impishly from inside Magician's stall.

Liz laughed. "That's not a bad idea!"

"When should I try and ride her, Liz?" Kerry asked. She was itching to find out whether her new horse was saddle-trained.

"Don't rush it," Liz replied patiently. "You've got all the time in the world."

No, I don't, Kerry thought. Not if I'm going to be ready for the next horse show. She hadn't told Liz yet that she was planning to ride Tapestry at the Winchester Charity Horse Show.

As soon as the vet had examined Tapestry and given Kerry detailed instructions on the mare's diet, Kerry took Liz's advice. She spent almost twenty-four hours a day with the mare for the next week. She even slept in the barn on a folding cot a couple of times.

Accompanied by Holly and Magician, Kerry patiently led Tapestry around the stable buildings and introduced her to her new surroundings. At first Tapestry was frightened of almost everything, including the small family of barn cats that skittered bravely under her hooves. She shied away from ordinary things like wheelbarrows and trash cans and almost jumped out of her skin when a couple of motorcycles roared down the lane.

When she wasn't taking Tapestry for long walks, Kerry was either grooming her or cleaning out her stall. The mare soon got used to having her around and actually started to whinny whenever Kerry entered the barn. Kerry knew she was finally beginning to gain the horse's trust.

Finally Kerry started lunging Tapestry in the indoor arena. With the mare at the end of a long lungeline, Kerry got her to walk and trot around her in a big circle. She was pleased with the progress so far, but it wasn't enough. They were going to have to work hard and fast if they hoped to be ready for the show.

"She's looking good!" Liz called out from the edge of the ring. "You ought to get a good price for her, and then you can get yourself what you really want."

"I've already got what I want," Kerry said to herself as Tapestry circled around her. The mare's golden coat shone softly in the filtered light, and her silvery mane and tail streamed out behind her. She was starting to fill out and had lost that hollow, half-starved look.

Liz ducked under the rail and joined Kerry in the middle of the arena. "Have you written your father about Tapestry yet?" she asked.

Kerry felt herself blushing. She'd tried several times to write, but so far all the letters had ended up in the wastebasket. She knew she was postponing the inevitable, but she was scared. Suppose he agreed with Liz and made her sell Tapestry?

Liz looked at her inquiringly. "Well, have you?"

Kerry shortened her hold on the lungeline and pulled Tapestry toward her. "Uh-uh," she muttered. Then she had a flash of inspiration. "Liz, would you write and tell him for me?"

Liz looked at her in astonishment. "But, Kerry, that's your responsibility." And as Kerry's blush deepened, Liz began to realize that Ben Logan might not be too thrilled with the news of Kerry's new horse. "You told me your father wouldn't mind if you bought a horse, Kerry. Remember?"

"I know, Liz," Kerry said, "and I'm sure he'll be okay about it, but it's just that—"

Liz looked at the girl's embarrassed face, then glanced toward Tapestry. Maybe if she wrote and told Ben Logan that Kerry had a good chance of improving the horse and selling her, it would soften the blow. "All right," she finally agreed, "I'll write to him."

49

"Hey, thanks, Liz!" Kerry said gratefully. She patted Tapestry's neck. "When should I start riding her?"

"Let's try putting a saddle on her first," Liz replied. "But not in here. We'll do it in the barn."

Kerry led Tapestry back into the stables and tied her up in the crossties. Magician stuck his nose over his stall door and neighed softly.

"She'll be fine as long as he's around," Holly said as Liz approached with a saddle over her arm. "She's nuts about him!"

Kerry showed the saddle to Tapestry, letting her sniff it all over before attempting to place it on her back. The mare stiffened slightly when she felt its weight. But with a few calm words from Kerry, she relaxed.

"Lead her around for a while," Liz suggested. "Let her get used to it."

As Kerry led Tapestry up the aisle, she glanced into Astronaut's stall. Whitney's handsome bay horse looked bored to death, and no wonder. His owner hadn't been anywhere near the barn since her cousin arrived. Kerry shook her head. How could anyone ignore a horse like that?

Once outside, Tapestry soon forgot about the saddle on her back. She happily followed Kerry all over the stable yard. By the time they returned to the barn, Liz declared it was time to try the bridle.

Kerry repeated the "show-and-tell" performance, letting Tapestry see the bridle before she tried to slip it on her head. After a few fumbling attempts, the mare finally opened her mouth and accepted the bit.

Kerry quickly adjusted the straps and buckles, making sure it was a good fit.

"Now what?" she asked Liz. "Should I try and get on her back?"

"No. Just lean your weight across her, a little at a time, while Holly and I hold her head."

Tapestry flinched when she felt Kerry's weight. Kerry pulled away and tried again. Gradually the mare relaxed. After twenty minutes she didn't seem to mind Kerry's weight at all.

"I think it's safe to say that she's been saddle-trained," Liz observed. "But we don't want to take any chances, Kerry. I think this is enough for one day. Besides, I need you two to run a few errands for me, okay?"

"Sure, Mom. What do you want us to do?" Holly asked.

Liz handed her a slip of paper. "I need a few things at the hardware store. I can't go to the village myself because I have a riding lesson in ten minutes. So just ride your bikes down for me and pick them up, okay?"

Kerry and Holly ran right into Whitney and her cousin as they left the hardware store.

"My mother's going to see Liz today about getting rid of that stupid horse of yours," Whitney said with a sneer.

Kerry reached for her bicycle, choking back a flood of angry words. It wouldn't do any good to have a fight with Whitney right in the middle of the village.

"Come on, Whitney!" Angela muttered impatiently. She shifted her pink and white shopping bag to her other arm and grabbed her cousin's arm. "Let's go home! I'm dying to try on my new sweater."

The two girls linked arms and sauntered down the narrow sidewalk, giggling.

"Don't let her get to you," Holly whispered urgently as Angela and Whitney disappeared around the corner.

"How does *she* know what Tapestry looks like now?" Kerry muttered angrily. She swung her leg over the bike and looked desperately at Holly. "She hasn't been anywhere near the barn since Angela arrived."

As they rode back up the hill toward the stables, Kerry could think of nothing else. "If my horse isn't in the barn when I get back," she said angrily to Holly, "I'm going to strangle Whitney with a pair of her argyle knee socks!"

"Stop worrying," Holly replied. "You know Mom won't listen to her."

Mrs. Myers's silver Mercedes was parked in the stable driveway when they got back to the barn. The sight of the car set Kerry's teeth on edge. She felt even worse when she ran into the stables and saw that Whitney and Angela were also there. Angela still had her shopping bag with her, and it was obvious she was still impatient to get back to the Myerses' house.

As soon as Kerry and Holly entered the barn, Mrs. Myers turned angrily toward Liz. "Liz, I want to see the awful horse that Kerry Logan owns," she said in a cold voice. "Whitney says it's a disgrace to the stables."

Liz frowned at Kerry, warning her not to interfere. Then she politely told Mrs. Myers to come with her to the stalls. The four girls followed a few feet behind. Kerry did her best to ignore Whitney's sneering face.

"Oh, who's that pretty little horse?" Mrs. Myers suddenly exclaimed when she and Liz reached Tapestry's stall.

"Mother! How could you?" Whitney screamed.

Holly stifled a burst of giggles by covering her mouth with both hands. Kerry caught the amused expression on Liz's face and said nothing at all.

"Now, where is *Kerry's* horse?" Mrs. Myers demanded. She glanced once more into Tapestry's stall and then looked expectantly toward Liz.

"She's right here, Mrs. Myers," Liz said, trying to hide the note of delicious triumph in her voice. "This is Tapestry."

"But Whitney said—" And then Mrs. Myers's voice faltered in confusion as she stared first at Kerry's new horse, then at Liz's smiling face.

"Let *me* see her!" Whitney pushed rudely past her mother and Liz. Her mouth fell wide open when she saw Tapestry's softly gleaming chestnut coat and her silvery blond mane and tail.

"Maybe you should come to the barn more often," Liz said to her in a neutral voice. "Then you'd know what Tapestry looks like *now*."

"Whitney, I don't understand what's going on," Mrs. Myers protested angrily. "I thought you said Kerry's horse was filthy dirty and nothing more than a bag of bones."

Holly's giggles finally erupted loudly, and Kerry couldn't help smiling. Mrs. Myers didn't know any-

54

thing about horses, and she depended on Whitney to keep her informed about what was happening at the stables. This time Whitney's information had backfired on both of them. There was no way Mrs. Myers could object to her horse now.

"Come on, Angela. Let's get out of here," Whitney snarled angrily. She glared at her bewildered mother and pulled her cousin roughly out of the barn behind her. Mrs. Myers looked slightly embarrassed, and she shrugged at Liz. Then completely ignoring Kerry and Holly, she strode out of the barn.

As soon as they'd gone, Liz, Holly, and Kerry broke out laughing. "That was the funniest thing I've seen in years," Liz gasped out. She was laughing so hard, she had to lean against the stall door for support.

Holly sat down on Magician's tack trunk, too convulsed with giggles to even speak. Kerry felt as if an enormous weight had been lifted from her shoulders. With Mrs. Myers's threat to evict Tapestry from the barn gone, she could really throw herself into getting her ready for the upcoming horse show. The Timber Ridge riding team was going to compete with only four riders. And with Tapestry's arrival at the barn, Liz now had six horses as well as six riders to choose from.

Kerry was more determined than ever that she and Tapestry would be one of the four pairs chosen. She had to prove to Liz—and everyone else—that she hadn't made a huge mistake in buying the mare.

Chapter Seven

"I'm going to practice over some jumps," Holly announced loudly from Magician's stall. "Want to come and help me?"

Kerry propped the pitchfork against the wall and rubbed her aching back. She was stripping the soiled bedding out of Tapestry's stall, and it was hard work!

"Sure," she agreed. She'd turned Tapestry outside in one of the small paddocks while she cleaned her stall. Later, she was planning on riding her for the first time.

Holly led Magician into the aisle, and Kerry followed them toward the outdoor jumping ring. Tapestry neighed loudly from the paddock as soon as she saw Magician.

"Oh, Kerry! Look at her! Doesn't she look terrific?" Holly exclaimed as the chestnut mare came galloping toward them.

With her silvery mane and tail flowing behind her

in the breeze, Tapestry charged up to the fence. She skidded to a stop, sending a shower of dirt and grass out from under her flashing hooves.

Kerry stopped to admire her. She really did look wonderful now—all cleaned up and shining brilliantly in the afternoon sun. Her muscles were starting to develop, and she looked nothing like the dirty, half-starved animal that Kerry had rescued.

"No, you can't come with us," Kerry said to her gently as she patted her nose through the fence rails. "I'll come and get you in a little while." And then we're going riding, she added to herself as she walked away toward the jumping ring that bordered Tapestry's paddock.

While Holly and Magician warmed up, Tapestry ran up and down along the fence, neighing constantly.

"I think she wants to join us," Kerry called out as Holly and Magician cantered over a jump. "Listen to her."

"So why don't you let her," Holly suggested. She trotted up to Kerry and grinned at her. "Bring her in here. She can run around while Magician and I practice."

"Good idea!" Kerry ran back to the barn for Tapestry's halter and leadrope. But when she got back outside, it looked as if Tapestry was going to take care of the situation by herself.

"No!" Kerry shrieked. She ran toward the paddock as fast as she could. "You can't jump that! It's too high!"

Her words were lost in the wind as the mare galloped past her. With her head held high and nostrils flaring, Tapestry charged toward the fence that separated her from her beloved Magician. It was over four feet high. And before Kerry had time to head her away, the mare gathered herself up and soared gracefully over the fence.

Kerry was so astonished, all she could do was stand and stare at her departing horse, now happily trotting toward Holly and Magician.

"Did you see that?" Holly cried. "That was *incredible*!" She reached out and patted Tapestry's nose. "You're quite a jumper, aren't you?"

Kerry ran up breathlessly, the empty halter swinging over her shoulder. She quickly slipped it over Tapestry's head, then flung her arms around the mare's neck. "I don't believe it," she said softly into her mane. "If I hadn't seen you jump that fence, I'd never have believed you could do it."

"Well, that answers one question," Holly declared triumphantly. "Now we know she can jump!"

"And how!" Kerry agreed enthusiastically. "Now all I have to do is find out if she'll do it with me on her back!"

"Wait till Mom hears about this!" Holly said with a laugh. "She'll think we're making it up." She wheeled Magician away and turned him toward the jumps in the middle of the ring. Kerry stood quietly beside Tapestry and watched as her friend expertly took the big black horse over the course.

As soon as Holly was finished, she cooled Magician off and put him back in his stall. Kerry gently placed the saddle on Tapestry's back, adjusted the bridle to fit her, and led her into the aisle. "I guess

we ought to do this in the indoor arena," she said nervously.

"Yeah. If she bucks you off, it won't hurt so much," Holly said helpfully. "Come on. I'll give you a hand."

The two girls led the mare into the empty arena. Kerry was relieved that no one else was using it. She didn't want a critical audience watching her first attempts at riding her new horse. "Maybe we ought to wait for your mother," she said as Holly took hold of Tapestry's reins.

"She's gone to get some hay," Holly replied. "She won't be back till suppertime. Come on. We know what we're doing."

Kerry cautiously placed her hands on the saddle and put her foot in the stirrup. Tapestry tried to move away from her, but Holly held her firm.

"Easy girl," Kerry said softly as she tried again. This time the mare didn't move. With one fluid movement Kerry gently lifted herself over the mare's back and sat carefully in the saddle.

"How does it feel?" Holly asked with a grin.

"Terrific!" Kerry breathed out slowly. She reached down and took hold of the reins while Holly clipped the lungeline to the special noseband on Tapestry's bridle.

Kerry squeezed the mare gently with her legs and told her to "walk on." Tapestry slowly circled around Holly, her ears twitching back and forth as if she wasn't too sure whether she approved of this or not.

"She's obviously been saddle-trained," Holly called out.

"Yeah," Kerry replied with relief. Now the next

question was, how much saddle-training had the mare actually had?

After several easy circles Kerry told Tapestry to trot. Without a moment's hesitation the mare broke into a slow, comfortable four-beat gait. Kerry sat firmly in the saddle while an immense feeling of joy and satisfaction flooded through her.

This was finally it! She was riding her very own horse. It was the most wonderful feeling in the world.

Kerry's excitement level rose. She tightened her hold on the reins and sat firmly in the saddle. Tapestry responded to her signals like clockwork and took off in a canter. At first her movements were rough and jerky. But Kerry worked hard with her hands, legs, and body the way she'd been trained to do, and Tapestry adjusted her stride.

"Her nose is too high," Holly said critically. "Give her more leg."

"You sound like your mother!" Kerry yelled back.

While Kerry's attention was momentarily diverted by Holly, the mare dropped her head, squealed, and bucked playfully. Kerry lost her stirrups and went sailing over Tapestry's head. She landed on the soft tanbark to the sound of Holly's pealing laughter.

"That'll teach you!" Holly cried as she pulled the still bucking horse into a smaller circle.

Kerry's face was red when she stood up and brushed the tanbark off her jeans. "That was pretty dumb," she chided herself. Grinning foolishly, she approached Tapestry and talked to her gently. "Calm down, girl. Playtime's over."

"Terrific new horse you've got there!" a scornful

voice rang out across the arena, its unwelcome sound echoing off the rafters. "Maybe you should enter her in a rodeo!"

Kerry groaned and turned round. Whitney and Angela were leaning over the rails, watching them closely. It was obvious they'd seen her get bucked off.

"I guess you *never* fall off!" Holly snapped back sarcastically as she helped Kerry back into the saddle.

"Never!" Whitney replied, and she nudged Angela sharply in the ribs.

"I went to a rodeo once," Angela said loudly. "I bet Kerry's horse would do real well out West!"

Whitney giggled. Then with another scornful look toward Kerry and Tapestry, she led her cousin toward the stables.

"Don't pay any attention to her," Holly warned as Kerry adjusted her stirrups. "Pretend she's not here."

Patiently and carefully, Kerry walked and trotted Tapestry on the lungeline, and finally got her to canter without bucking. "I think we're ready to go solo," she said to Holly after another twenty minutes.

Holly released the lungeline's clip. As she coiled the long, webbed line into a circle, she smiled to herself. Kerry and Tapestry were going to do just fine together as long as they didn't rush things. Holly knew how much Kerry wanted to be on the riding team for the next horse show, and she crossed her fingers. They had to make it. After all this work and trouble, Kerry would be devastated if she wasn't picked for the team.

Chapter Eight

Kerry spent every available minute with Tapestry. Under Liz's critical eye, she practiced and practiced, building up Tapestry's muscles until her own were screaming for mercy. Liz had been almost unbelieving when Kerry told her about Tapestry's incredible jump over the paddock fence.

"I think you're putting me on," Liz said with a smile. "Not even Magician has tried to jump that fence."

"Just you wait, Mom," Holly warned. "When Kerry starts jumping that horse, you'll believe us. Tapestry's a natural."

After hours and hours of patient schooling on the flat, Kerry finally decided that Tapestry was ready for a small jump. Holly adjusted the height of the cross-rails in the middle of the ring so that it was no more than eighteen inches high. "That ought to do it," she said with a smile.

"Kiddy jumps!" Whitney said scornfully as she rode past on Astronaut.

Kerry glared at her. She wished Whitney hadn't chosen today to finally start practicing for the horse show. Astronaut was nervous and edgy, and his rider was having a hard time keeping him under control. She saw Angela Pearson straddled on the paddock fence, looking bored to death. Angela hated hanging around at the barn, so Kerry knew Whitney wouldn't ride for long. She was right. After a couple of turns around the jumping course, Whitney declared she didn't need any more practice. "I'll make the team," she said with a sneer as she left the ring. "But you won't, Kerry Logan. Not on that fleabag horse of yours."

"Just you wait and see!" Kerry snapped. She turned away from the departing horse and rider and forced herself to concentrate on Tapestry.

At first Kerry trotted Tapestry over the Cavelettis—sturdy wooden poles, lying on the ground—just to warm her up and loosen her muscles. Then she turned toward the cross-rail and trotted slowly over it.

"That looked simple," Holly said. "She's obviously done this before."

"Right," Kerry agreed. "Today the cross-rails—tomorrow the paddock fence!"

Holly gradually raised the height of the cross-rail until Tapestry was jumping it at almost three feet. The mare appeared to really enjoy herself going over the jump. With each successful try Kerry's confidence about making the riding team grew. She couldn't believe her luck! She'd found a horse for only forty-five dollars who *loved* to jump as much as she did.

Liz's praise was loud and vocal. "That mare's a natural jumper," she said approvingly as Kerry cantered Tapestry over the cross-rail for her. "I believe you now about the paddock fence. It's the way she moves. She's very graceful."

Kerry felt warm inside at the praise. Now maybe Liz wouldn't press her to consider selling the horse. All the money in the world wouldn't induce her to sell Tapestry!

"Mom, when are you going to pick the team?" Holly asked.

"I'm not," Liz replied.

"Why not?" Holly was shocked.

"Because with you trying out, someone's sure to yell 'favoritism' if you get picked."

"So who's going to do it then?" Holly asked.

"I've asked Madge Parker to come up next week to put you all through your paces. I'm staying well away from this one."

Kerry was overjoyed to hear Liz's news. Madge Parker was an old family friend, and Kerry liked her very much. Madge had once owned a breeding farm but now spent most of her time writing mysteries. She was lots of fun and an excellent judge of horses and riders. Kerry knew she'd pick the team fairly.

"Do you think Whitney will make it?" she asked Holly as they put their horses in the barn. Tapestry was still slightly sweaty, and Kerry brushed her vigorously with a stiff brush.

65

"I hope not," Holly muttered as she took Magician's saddle and bridle off. "She doesn't deserve to make it. She's only practiced once in the last month."

Kerry wasn't sure if she wanted Whitney on the team or not. On the one hand, it would be relaxing to go to a horse show without the aggravation of Whitney being around. But she wanted the chance to compete against her— and beat her. Kerry was sure she could do it.

A few days before the team tryouts, Kerry decided it was time to take her new horse out trail riding. So far, all of Tapestry's training had been in the riding ring, and Kerry knew how much the mare would enjoy the freedom of the woods and trails.

She and Holly set off one afternoon and headed toward the cross-country course. Holly was going to take Magician over some of the jumps. Kerry was itching to join her, but she knew Tapestry wasn't ready for the challenge of the demanding cross-country course yet.

As they cantered along the trail, Kerry felt as if she'd never been happier. She was riding her very own horse, accompanied by her best friend, and looking forward to an exciting horse show. If only her father could be home to see it.

Thinking about her father turned Kerry's attention toward her unsettled future, and her good mood dimmed. It was impossible to imagine life without Tapestry; Kerry felt as if she'd owned her forever. The pretty chestnut mare had become the most important thing in her life. Yet it could all end when her father returned. He'd already written to say that he would reserve judgment on her new horse until he got back from the Middle East, and she was worried about his reaction to the newcomer in her life.

Holly and Magician disappeared into the woods to jump the cross-country course, leaving Kerry deep in thought about her father's latest letter. He'd said his company was thinking about transferring him to a new office, but he didn't say where it was. Suppose they had to live in a city! Where would she keep Tapestry? Did they have boarding stables in places like Boston, or even New York? And even if they did, would her father be willing to pay for Tapestry's upkeep? Kerry shuddered, knowing she'd never be able to earn enough money to pay for it herself, even if she worked at two jobs. And her father would never go for that. As far as he was concerned, school came first.

Tapestry snorted impatiently, and Kerry pulled her mind back to the present. It wouldn't do any good to stew over the unknown.

"Come on, girl. Let's try the jumps," she said quietly as she urged the mare toward the small course of fences that the cross-country riders used for practice.

Tapestry jumped easily over the small brush jump and the rustic poles. Kerry ended the jumps with a feeling of exhilaration she hadn't felt when they jumped in the riding ring back at the stables.

Just before Holly returned, a small group of people entered the meadow carrying camera equipment. Kerry stared at them curiously as they set up tripods and started to take pictures of the scenery. Slowly she approached the group.

A red-haired young woman looked up and smiled at her. "Hi, that's a pretty horse you've got there."

The woman introduced herself as Janet MacIntosh, and said she was taking a series of photographs for a local magazine. "Say, how'd you like to be in one of them?" she suggested casually as Holly and Magician rode out of the woods. "You and your friend on that black horse. That'd be perfect for my story!"

While Janet and her associates chose the right background, Holly and Kerry giggled together at the prospect of appearing in a magazine. "Won't Whitney be jealous," Holly muttered as the camera crew showed them where to stand.

Janet MacIntosh took half a roll of film of the two girls on horseback. When she finished, she started asking questions. She was delighted when Kerry told her about Tapestry's rescue from the horse auction. "You're sure you don't mind if I include that in my article?" she asked before they packed up and left the meadow.

Kerry shook her head. She was very proud of her horse, and she asked when the magazine would be out.

"Next week, if I hustle!" Janet MacIntosh replied. "You can get a copy in the village."

Kerry and Holly rode back to the barn, talking happily about the unexpected meeting with Janet, and the upcoming riding tryouts. "How do you feel about your chances now?" Holly asked as they approached the stables.

"Pretty good," Kerry said. "Tapestry loves to jump. As long as Magician's around, I don't think she'll be nervous at the show."

"Well, you'd better hope I make the team, then," Holly replied with a grin. "Otherwise, you're sunk!"

"Don't be dumb! Of course you'll make it," Kerry said quickly. "You're a fantastic rider."

"*Was* a fantastic rider," Holly murmured quietly. "I'm getting better, but I've still got a long way to go."

Holly's subdued words stayed with Kerry as she got busy cleaning up her horse after the ride. Holly just *had* to make the team. It wouldn't be the same unless they were both competing, *and* beating Whitney Myers as well.

Madge Parker arrived the night before the team tryouts, and Kerry and Holly greeted her with yelps of laughter and affection. The tall, gray-haired woman scooped them both into her arms and gave them an enormous hug. "I've missed you two young scamps," she said with a twinkle in her eye. "And from what Liz tells me, you've got some great news, Kerry."

Kerry happily told Madge all about her new horse, and Madge insisted on going out to the barn right away to see for herself.

"You were absolutely right!" she exclaimed when Kerry introduced her to Tapestry. "She's quite a beauty. Still too thin, mind you, but if I'm not mistaken, you've got yourself a fine horse."

Tapestry's proud owner smiled happily to herself as Madge inspected the mare from top to bottom.

"Keep working her, Kerry," Madge said as she patted Tapestry's neck. "She still needs a lot more muscling up, but she's got great potential. Her legs are strong, and she's got good bone structure. I bet she loves to jump."

Holly interrupted with the story of Tapestry and the paddock fence, and Madge laughed. "I'm looking forward to seeing her jump tomorrow," she said as she left the stall. "And good luck to both of you. I won't play favorites, so you've got to earn your place on the team."

By ten o'clock the next morning, the horses and riders were in the ring. There were only five, instead of the anticipated six, since Jennifer McKenna's horse, Prince, was lame and couldn't be ridden. Jennifer, looking very disappointed, was sitting on the fence beside Angela.

Kerry smiled when she saw Whitney's look of horror as Madge announced that part of the selection process involved having a clean horse and clean tack. Madge then inspected each horse and rider, and made lots of notes on the clipboard she was carrying.

"It's not fair," Whitney grumbled. "Having a clean saddle doesn't make you a better rider."

"What's wrong, Whitney?" Holly drawled in an innocent voice. "Isn't Angela any good at cleaning tack?"

Kerry almost choked as she tried to stop from laughing out loud at the image of prissy Angela Pearson cleaning Whitney's grubby saddle and bridle. But she wouldn't have been that surprised if Whitney had conned her cousin into doing the job.

Whitney hated to clean her own tack and was very good at getting her endless string of "best friends" to do it for her.

Whitney's face clouded over and she glared angrily at Holly. It was a good thing Madge didn't see her. She was even more of a stickler about good sportsmanship than she was about cleanliness.

Madge told them to spread out around the outside of the ring. And for the next fifteen minutes they all walked, trotted, and cantered at her command. Then they reversed direction and did it again.

"This is getting boring," Whitney muttered loudly as she rode past Angela.

"Okay, kids," Madge called out. "Line up. It's time for the jumping."

"Now maybe Whitney will get over being bored," Holly remarked as she rode up next to Kerry. Magician whinnied at Tapestry, and Holly had to pull his head away from his special friend. He was much more interested in chewing on her mane than standing still.

One by one the riders took their horses over the jumps. Robin Lovell had a perfect round, and so did Sue Armstrong on her pretty, dapple-gray mare, Tara. Holly and Magician went next, and the black horse soared over the jumps as if they were nothing more than a collection of shoe boxes. Holly was smiling when she rejoined Kerry in the middle of the ring.

"Okay, Kerry. Your turn."

Kerry's stomach tightened into a knot, and she tried to relax. It wouldn't do any good to let Tapestry know she was nervous. She cantered in a big circle at the end of the arena and turned toward the first jump. Tapestry popped over the cross-rail easily. The parallel bars were next. As they went over them, Tapestry's hind foot caught one of the poles. It shuddered violently but didn't fall down.

She cleared the brush jump, then Kerry turned the corner to face the tricky in-and-out. She had to pace her horse carefully so that Tapestry would only take two strides between the two fences. If she didn't time it right, the horse might try for an extra stride and possibly crash into the second jump.

"One, two, three . . . and up," Kerry counted softly to herself as they flew over the first jump. Tapestry took the required two strides, and they flew effortlessly over the second fence. Kerry allowed herself a sigh of relief. Only the wall was left. She hadn't jumped Tapestry over it before; and as they approached the forbidding red jump, she could feel the mare's hesitation. "Go on, girl! You can do it!" Kerry leaned forward. She squeezed her gently with her legs, and the mare took off in a gigantic leap. They cleared the wall with plenty of room to spare.

Holly was smiling and clapping her hands when Kerry rode up to her. "That looked *great*!" she said enthusiastically. "Now you can relax and watch Whitney foul things up. Astronaut's not in a very good mood today, and she's having a hard time with him."

"I'm not surprised," Kerry muttered. Ever since Angela Pearson had arrived, Whitney hadn't exercised her horse more than twice. And although Astronaut was well trained, he was an energetic horse and needed lots of riding to keep him well behaved.

Whitney somehow got her hyperactive horse around the course, but not without a few near disasters. Astronaut managed to put an extra stride between the in-and-out, and he popped over the second fence like a cat. He jumped straight up in the air, and Whitney almost fell off. Then he tried to refuse at the wall. But Whitney whacked him so hard with her crop he blundered over it, knocking three bricks down.

"Look out! She can't stop him!" Kerry cried as Whitney and Astronaut thundered toward them.

"Watch out, Whitney!" Madge yelled. But it was too late. The out-of-control horse ran right into Tally Ho. As Robin frantically tried to get her horse out of the way, Astronaut kicked out sideways, and one of his hooves slammed right into Tally Ho's shoulder.

Madge glared at Whitney as she ran up to see what damage had been done. Robin had dismounted immediately, and Kerry heard her cry out. It was obvious that something was wrong.

"It's not serious," Madge said with relief as she examined the small gash opened by Astronaut's hoof. "A few inches lower, and you'd have been in trouble." She straightened up and waved toward Liz. "You'd better call the vet. We're going to need some stitches."

Robin looked utterly miserable. She asked Madge if Tally Ho would be better in time for the horse show.

"That's for the vet to decide," Madge said kindly. Then she turned toward the rest of the riders. "Okay, kids. That's it. Put your horses away, and Liz will give you the results later on."

"I could kill Whitney," Holly said angrily as she settled Magician back in his stall. "It's all her fault. If she'd ridden Astronaut more, this would never have happened."

"Think she'll make the team?" Kerry asked with a grin.

Holly shot her an exasperated look and disappeared into Magician's stall. A few minutes later Kerry was pleased to hear Madge chewing out Whitney in Liz's office. Angela was hanging around the doorway, and for once she wasn't smiling.

"I wonder what excuse Whitney will give her mother when she isn't picked for the team," Holly muttered as she and Kerry left the barn.

Kerry stopped in her tracks. Suddenly what had just happened sunk in. "You know," she said slowly as the reality of it dawned on her, "if Tally Ho can't be ridden in the show, Whitney will make the team!"

Holly groaned. "You're right! Whitney *will* win by default. With Tally Ho *and* Prince out of the action, there's only four of us left."

Much as Kerry felt sorry for both Robin and Jennifer, she was secretly glad that Whitney would be riding against her. Judging from Astronaut's behavior in the jumping ring, he and Whitney shouldn't be too hard to beat. It was something she dreamed about . . . riding her very own horse and beating Whitney Myers once and for all!

Chapter Nine

Kerry felt a sense of anticlimax when Liz announced the results of the riding team selection trials. Since the barn's veterinarian had grounded Robin's horse for three weeks, that left only four riders—Holly, Sue, Whitney, and herself. So, Liz's announcement came as no surprise. Except that Whitney behaved as though her superior riding skills had won her a place on the team.

"I told you I'd be picked," she said in a smug voice to her cousin.

"You're such a terrific rider," Angela replied smoothly. "You're the best one here!"

Holly almost gagged. After the two girls had left the barn, she spouted her indignation to everyone who was left in Liz's small office. "It's not fair," she grumbled. "Whitney only made the team because Astronaut kicked Tally Ho. Why don't you let Robin ride Astronaut instead!"

Liz gently told her daughter to leave the running of the riding team to her. Then she handed out the class prize lists for the horse show and told the girls to start practicing.

Kerry and Holly quickly read the list of classes offered and the rules for competing with a team. "It says we can choose two classes, and they don't all have to be the same ones," Holly said.

"Yes," her mother explained. "This show's quite different from the ones you're used to. As a team, each of you gets to choose which two classes you want to enter. The team racking up the most points is the winner. The classes are rated by difficulty, and you get more team points for winning in one of the harder classes."

"Great!" Kerry said. "That way we can choose what we're best at."

"That's right," Liz replied. "Now I want all of you to let me know by tomorrow which two you'll be entering. Choose carefully. Pick the classes you feel confident about." She got up and went to look for Whitney so she could give her a prize list as well.

"I'm going to try for Gambler's Choice," Holly said as she stared at the piece of paper in her hands. "It's got a high rating. So if I win a ribbon, we'll get more points for the team!"

"Hmmm," Kerry said thoughtfully. "I think Tapestry would do well in the Pleasure Horse class, don't you?"

Holly nodded. "Are you going to enter the Junior Open Jumping?"

"You bet," Kerry said quickly. She knew Whitney

would be sure to pick that class, and she wanted to be in it as well.

Holly laughed, knowing exactly what Kerry was thinking. "Why don't you wait till Whitney's given Mom her choices before you make up your mind," she advised with a knowing smile. "You don't want to miss the chance of beating her!"

Kerry couldn't help feeling excited. The show was getting closer, and it was all she could think about. Holly had definitely made up her mind about the classes she was going to enter. Gambler's Choice was an exciting event to watch. Each rider picked his or her own route over the jumping course, and the one who rode it the fastest with the least amount of faults was the winner. Magician was terrific at taking tight turns and leaping over jumps from impossible angles. She figured Holly would do well in that class.

As soon as Kerry found out that Whitney had chosen the Junior Open Jumping and the Junior Equitation class, Kerry made her decision. She would enter the Pleasure Horse class and the same jumping class as Whitney. The thought of challenging Whitney over a jumping course in front of a large audience was irresistible. She only hoped she wasn't making a terrible mistake. After all, this was Tapestry's first horse show.

Riding team practice sessions swung into high gear as the day of the horse show grew closer. Liz patiently coaxed and cajoled her team of young riders to a high level of proficiency. They practiced on the flat—walking, trotting, and cantering before Liz's critical eye—until Kerry felt she could ride with her hands behind her back!

At least once every day they spent two hours in the outside jumping ring, taking turns riding the course of jumps that Liz set up for them. Holly and Magician practiced for the Gambler's Choice, taking small, tight turns and jumping the fences from almost impossible angles. Even Whitney worked hard. In fact, more than once Liz had to caution her about riding too much.

"That horse will go sour on you," she said firmly as Whitney cantered by on a very sweaty Astronaut. "Ease up a bit, and take him for a trail ride!"

"I know what I'm doing!" Whitney shot back angrily. With a defiant look at Liz she pulled Astronaut around to face the parallel bars. The horse was obviously tired, and he stumbled as he approached the fence. Whitney raked at his sides with her heels and forced him over the jump.

"You won't have any trouble beating her," Holly whispered to Kerry as Astronaut's hind foot touched one of the poles. It wobbled violently and crashed to the ground.

Kerry hoped she was right. Astronaut was behaving badly, and no wonder! Whitney was pushing him too hard, and Kerry knew why. Whitney was determined to win the coveted blue ribbon in the Junior Open Jumping.

The lesson ended, and the four exhausted riders walked their horses back to the barn. Kerry tried to ignore her aching muscles as she brushed the sweat off Tapestry's back. A surge of affection for the gallant little mare flooded through her, and she wound her arms around Tapestry's warm neck and hugged her.

"Kerry, where are you?" Liz's voice called from the other end of the barn.

Kerry disentangled herself from Tapestry's mane. "I'm in here!" she yelled back.

A minute later Liz poked her head around the stall door. She had a worried frown on her face, and Kerry wondered what was wrong.

"Come into my office," Liz said. "We have to talk."

Kerry's heart started to thump loudly. This sounded awful! She hoped it wasn't a letter from her father announcing a move. With a terrible sinking feeling she followed Liz back down the aisle.

Once they were both inside the tiny office, Liz swung the door shut and looked closely at Kerry. "I don't really know how to tell you this," she began.

Kerry's heart almost stopped beating. Liz's words sounded so ominous. She started to panic. "What's the matter?" she choked out.

"I've just had a very disturbing phone call," Liz said quietly. "It seems Tapestry may be a stolen horse!"

For a moment or two Liz's words didn't register. "What—what did you say?" Kerry asked in a faint voice.

"A man just called and said he has a picture of Tapestry. He thinks she might belong to him. His mare was stolen from his farm—somewhere near Burlington, I think he said. Anyway, it's way north of here."

Kerry swallowed hard and shook her head. It

couldn't be true. This wasn't happening to her.

"This man—Mr. Hoffman—has that magazine picture of you and Tapestry," Liz explained gently. "He thinks she might be his missing horse."

"The magazine picture?" Kerry repeated, shaking her head slowly. She just couldn't believe it! Then she started to get angry—angry at herself for letting the woman in the meadow take their photograph. "If only I hadn't let them take that dumb picture," she said tearfully, "then this wouldn't have happened." She turned toward Liz. "Now what do we do, Liz? I can't just let some stranger walk in here and take Tapestry away. She's mine! I won't let her go!"

"Kerry," Liz replied gently. "This man's horse was stolen almost a year ago. Just think how you'd feel if your missing horse suddenly turned up. Wouldn't you want to check it out?"

Kerry tried to put herself in Mr. Hoffman's shoes, but it wasn't easy. All she could think about was losing her precious horse.

"Mr. Hoffman's coming by the stables tomorrow," Liz said. "Now, Kerry, don't get upset. He isn't sure about this since he's only got the magazine picture to go by."

"Tomorrow?" Kerry croaked. She forced herself to look at Liz. Then she burst into tears and buried her face in her hands.

Liz put her arms around Kerry's shoulders and hugged her. "Don't cry," she said soothingly. "I doubt Tapestry's his horse. There must be dozens of horses in Vermont who look like her."

All the excitement about the horse show suddenly

vanished. Kerry wished she could take Tapestry and run away and hide from the mysterious Mr. Hoffman. Between sniffs and tears she stumbled back into Tapestry's stall and hugged her horse fiercely. Her dream was disappearing. Tapestry was going to be taken away from her, and there was nothing she could do to stop it from happening.

Dimly she heard Holly enter the stall. "What's wrong?" Holly exclaimed when she saw Kerry's flushed, tear-streaked face. "You look terrible!"

Kerry wiped her eyes and fell into Holly's outstretched arms. "Oh, Holly," she wailed. "It's awful. I can't believe it's happening!"

"Can't believe *what's* happening?" Holly asked. She hugged her friend, and then pushed Kerry away from her. "Come on, you'd better tell me what's going on."

Between sniffs and a few stray tears, Kerry told Holly about Mr. Hoffman's phone call.

"I wonder where he got a copy of the magazine?" Holly mused thoughtfully. "I thought it was only a local thing. Didn't you say he was from somewhere up north?"

Kerry nodded. "Yes," she sniffed. "Burlington, I think."

"I sent that picture to Mr. Hoffman!"

Kerry turned around quickly and saw Whitney leaning over the stall door. "What did you say?" she asked incredulously.

"I said I sent him that picture," Whitney replied smoothly. "I thought it was only right. After all, his horse had been stolen, and its description matched Tapestry exactly."

82

Holly and Kerry stared open-mouthed at Whitney. Just as Kerry was about to explode with anger, Angela's face appeared beside Whitney.

"It was my idea," Angela said with a toss of her head. "I found a few 'Missing Horse' notices in one of Whitney's horse magazines. I suggested we send off your horse's photos in case she really belonged to someone else."

"You meddling—" Holly burst out furiously.

"I don't care what you call us," Whitney said in a stony voice. "I know we did the right thing." Her pale eyes flashed dangerously. "After all, Holly Chapman, how would *you* feel if your precious Magician was stolen. Wouldn't you want to know if there was a chance of getting him back?"

Holly bit her lip. All the nasty words she wanted to hurl at Whitney remained unspoken. The girl's comment had reminded her of how desperate she'd felt when her Magician had gotten out of his stall and for a few frantic days everyone assumed he'd been stolen.

"I bet you did this just to spite me," Kerry said in a carefully controlled voice. She glared at Whitney and Angela, her eyes never leaving their sneering faces. "You're afraid I'll beat you at the horse show, aren't you, Whitney?"

"Of course I'm not!" Whitney snapped. "My horse can beat your stupid animal any day!"

"Hah!" Holly snorted.

"Come on, Whitney," Angela interrupted. "Let's go to the club. The company's much better over there." She tugged at her cousin's arm and dragged her down the aisle.

"Just you wait, Whitney!" Holly cried. "Tapestry isn't Mr. Hoffman's horse. You've caused a lot of trouble for nothing, as usual!"

Whitney stopped and turned around. "Well, we'll just wait and see, won't we?" she said smoothly. "He'll be here tomorrow, and then you can say good-by to your precious horse, Kerry Logan. It's all over. She's not yours. She belongs to Mr. Hoffman!"

"I'm going to take Tapestry out trail riding all day tomorrow. Then Mr. Hoffman can't possibly see her!" Kerry said angrily as she watched Whitney and Angela walk away from them.

"Don't be a jerk!" Holly replied. "If you're not here tomorrow, he'll just come back another day. You'd better get it over with. Don't worry. I bet Tapestry isn't his horse."

Kerry wasn't reassured. Somehow she knew her run of good luck had finally come to an end, and it was all Whitney's fault. Tomorrow this unknown man would reclaim his long-lost horse, and Tapestry would be gone from her forever. She felt trapped. There wasn't anything she could do except hope for a miracle.

Chapter Ten

After a fitful night Kerry awoke the next morning to the sound of rain beating on her window. Feeling groggy and disoriented, she got out of bed and looked outside. She felt as gray as the weather.

Maybe Mr. Hoffman won't come in the rain, she thought as she pulled on a pair of jeans and a heavy sweater. Fat chance of that, she added, giving her sweater a tug. He's going to come and take my horse away.

Fighting back a flood of angry tears, Kerry silently went into the kitchen and fixed herself a bowl of cereal. Holly was still asleep, and from the empty coffee mug on the counter, it was obvious that Liz had already gone to the barn.

Kerry sat down at the table and picked at her food, her mind working furiously. Maybe Liz and Holly were right! After all, Mr. Hoffman hadn't seen his horse in over a year. It was possible that he was mistaken. She crossed her fingers. It was her only hope.

Tapestry whinnied happily when she heard Kerry's footsteps approaching her stall. "Hi, girl," Kerry muttered as she let herself inside. The mare whinnied again, and Kerry wrapped her arm around Tapestry's neck. She stroked her face gently. "I don't want to lose you," she said softly. The mare nudged her, as if she understood what Kerry was saying.

"I guess you can't hide Tapestry on the trails, huh?" Holly's cheerful voice suddenly interrupted the silence. "It's pouring buckets outside!"

Kerry looked up and saw her friend grinning at her from the doorway. She shook her head.

"Do you want to practice in the indoor arena with me?" Holly continued.

Kerry had lost all interest in the horse show. Somehow it seemed stupid and unimportant all of a sudden. She shrugged and went back to hugging Tapestry.

Holly sensed her mood immediately. "Come on. Stop moping. It won't solve anything. A good run at the jumps will take your mind off your problems!" She turned and went into Magician's stall, whistling cheerfully.

Kerry went through the motions of cleaning Tapestry's stall and getting ready for their morning ride. Liz had just finished with her first riding lesson, and the arena would be free for an hour until the next group of students arrived.

While Holly and Magician practiced over the jumping course, Kerry rode around the perimeter of the arena. She felt stiff and unbalanced, and knew she was riding badly. Tapestry, unused to a clumsy rider, kept stumbling, and her movements were rough and jerky. But Kerry couldn't help it. Every time she heard a car or a truck pull in the stables' driveway, she tensed up. Maybe *this* was the mysterious Mr. Hoffman.

By noon he still hadn't arrived, and Kerry's hopes started to rise. "Maybe he's changed his mind," she muttered to Holly as they shared a sandwich in Liz's office.

Holly swallowed a mouthful of food and glanced at the clock. "Plenty of time yet," she said.

"Big help you are!" Kerry snapped sharply.

Holly changed the subject. "Did you know Whitney's mother is part of the organizing committee for the horse show?"

Kerry shook her head.

"So if Whitney doesn't win, she'll be furious. This event is one of her favorite charities." Holly paused. "Hey," she said slowly, "if this Mr. Hoffman really does own Tapestry and takes her away, Mom will be short a rider for the team, won't she?"

Kerry glared at her. "Don't talk like that!" She felt close to tears, and Holly's flip remarks weren't helping.

"Sorry," Holly mumbled. "I wasn't thinking. Look, I'm sure he's wrong about Tapestry. I just know he is. I can feel it in my bones."

Kerry didn't trust Holly's bones. She had an awful feeling in the pit of her stomach that she was going to lose the one thing she loved most in the whole world. She looked at the clock again. As Holly said, there was still plenty of time.

Suddenly Whitney stuck her head around the door. "Are you two using the arena this afternoon? I want to practice." She looked scornfully at Kerry, hunched down on the tack trunk. "I'm glad your stupid horse is leaving. She's a disgrace to the barn."

"Get lost!" Holly snapped.

Whitney sneered at her. "We won't need Kerry Logan's help at the horse show, you know. The vet's going to check Tally Ho and Prince out tomorrow. One of them will probably be okay to ride."

Kerry bit her lip and said nothing. She wished there was something she could do to Whitney to pay her back for the misery and trouble she'd caused. Then Whitney's words sunk in. If it was true, then Liz would be able to compete with the team, regardless of whether Tapestry was around or not. She felt more miserable than ever.

Mr. Hoffman finally showed up at three o'clock. As soon as Kerry heard the car pulling into the driveway, she sensed the moment of truth was at hand. For an insane moment she was tempted to take Tapestry and make a mad dash for the woods. She didn't want to face Tapestry's former owner, if that's who he was.

She hid herself in Tapestry's stall, but a few minutes later she heard Liz calling her. Kerry stayed where she was, knowing Liz would find her.

Finally her curiosity got the better of her, and she stuck her head over the stall door. Liz was walking down the aisle, talking to a tall, thin man wearing a tan raincoat and heavy black boots. Drops of rain were clinging to the brim of his peaked cap. He was smiling as he and Liz approached the stall.

Kerry shrank back and leaned against Tapestry for support.

"Ah, there you are," Liz said in a strained voice. She swung the door open, and Mr. Hoffman followed her inside. "Kerry, this is Mr. Hoffman."

Kerry raised her eyes slowly and forced herself to be polite. "Hello," she muttered, moving even closer to Tapestry.

"I'm sorry to barge in on you like this," Mr. Hoffman apologized. He glanced at his watch. "I won't keep you long, because I have a business appointment and I'm already late." He approached Tapestry with his hand held out in front of him. Gently he stroked the mare's nose and then ran his hand down the crest of her neck. "This is quite remarkable," he said softly.

"Well?" Liz asked. She glanced nervously at Kerry.

Kerry kept her hand on Tapestry's neck and looked at Mr. Hoffman out of the corner of her eye. He wasn't quite the monster she'd been expecting. She noticed the careful and expert way he examined the horse—quietly and efficiently, with no sudden moves.

After what seemed an eternity during which none of them spoke, Mr. Hoffman finally turned to Kerry. "Mrs. Chapman filled me in on how you found this mare. You've done a remarkable job, young lady. You ought to be very proud of yourself."

Kerry bit her lip. The suspense was killing her. Why didn't he just get it over with and tell her whether Tapestry belonged to him or not. She

couldn't stand it much longer. "Is she yours?" she blurted out.

Mr. Hoffman smiled. "I think so, but I can't be one hundred percent sure. You see, it was over a year ago that Melody—that's the name we gave her—was stolen. This horse looks exactly like her." He gently opened Tapestry's mouth and looked at her teeth. "Yes, she'd be about the right age."

"How old was your mare?" Liz asked.

"Five. She'd be six years old by now," he replied.

"Do you have any photographs of her?"

Mr. Hoffman reached into his pocket and pulled out a brown envelope. Carefully he took out two color photographs. Kerry leaned forward to look at them. The first one showed a pretty little chestnut foal by its mother's side.

"That was taken when Melody was a few weeks old," Mr. Hoffman explained. Then he showed them the second photograph. Kerry and Liz both gasped in unison. It was Tapestry! No doubt about it. The resemblance was incredible.

Kerry turned away. She didn't want to cry in front of Mr. Hoffman. It took her a few seconds to gain control. Then she swung around to face them again. "Are you sure?" she whispered, hardly able to breathe.

Mr. Hoffman hesitated. "I'm awfully sorry about this, Kerry. Believe me, I hate to hurt you this way, but I'm pretty confident that this is our Melody. I'd like to pay you for rescuing her from the horse auction and for taking such good care of her."

"I don't want any money," Kerry said, her eyes

burning fiercely as she held back her tears.

"Kerry, don't be silly," Liz warned. "You can always buy another horse."

You don't understand! Kerry wanted to scream out. This is the horse I want. I don't want another one! But she remained silent.

Mr. Hoffman looked at his watch again. "I really have to leave now," he said. "I'll be away until the twenty-fifth. Then I'd like to come and get the mare, if that's all right with you."

"That's the day of the horse show!" Liz exclaimed.

"The Winchester Charity Horse Show?" Mr. Hoffman asked as he went toward the stall door.

Liz nodded.

Mr. Hoffman smiled. "Melody's a terrific show horse. She won lots of blue ribbons before she disappeared." He looked closely at Kerry. "I'm sure you've been looking forward to it, so why don't I come to the show and pick her up after you're all through?"

Kerry nodded. There was no point in telling him, or Liz, that she didn't even want to be in the show now. It had lost all its appeal.

"I'll see you at the show, then," Mr. Hoffman said as he went toward the stall door. His face softened into a sympathetic smile. "It's been such a long time since I saw Melody," he said. "When I see her in the show ring—in action—I'll know for sure that this is my Melody. Not that there's really any doubt in my mind."

Liz smiled weakly and led him back down the aisle. Kerry collapsed in a heap onto a pile of bedding. She sat there alone with her arms wound around her

93

knees, sobbing quietly. Holly found her there a few minutes later.

"I was in Magician's stall," Holly said softly as she sat down beside Kerry. "I thought it best if I stayed out of the way. I'm sorry. I know how you must feel."

"How could you know?" Kerry said miserably. "You've never lost your horse before." A large tear trickled down her face. "I'm going to lose Tapestry, and there's nothing I can do about it." She buried her face in her arms and sobbed. "I don't belong *anywhere!*"

Holly put her arm around Kerry's shoulders and hugged her. "Don't be dumb! You belong here, with Mom and me."

"I wish I did." Kerry wiped her face and sniffed loudly. "It's just that everything's such a mess. Tapestry was the only thing I really had, and now she's being taken away, too. I feel alone . . . and kind of lost. Am I making any sense?"

"No, you're not," Holly replied firmly. "Look, you've got Mom and me. You know how much we love you."

"Thanks," Kerry muttered as Holly gave her another hug. "I wish my dad were here," she added quietly as she buried her face in Holly's shoulder. "He'd think of a way to keep Tapestry—" And then she stopped. Her father hadn't even agreed to letting her keep Tapestry at all. Maybe he'd be pleased that Mr. Hoffman was going to take her away! She started to cry again. There was nothing she could do to change things. Tapestry would be hers until the horse show, and after that . . . she couldn't bear to think about it.

Chapter Eleven

Whitney's prediction that the vet would pronounce either Prince or Tally Ho fit enough to be ridden was wrong. Neither of the injured horses would make the horse show. Kerry had no choice but to ride.

"Come on, Kerry. Don't back out now," Holly said urgently. The two girls were sitting at the kitchen table, and Holly was studying the horse show prize list.

"I don't want to ride," Kerry mumbled quietly. She felt sick inside every time she thought of Mr. Hoffman coming with his horse trailer to take Tapestry away.

"Mom needs a full team. Besides, you want to beat Whitney, don't you?" Holly insisted.

Kerry hesitated. She'd been so worried about losing Tapestry that she'd forgotten all about wanting to beat Whitney Myers. It was still a tempting thought, especially after what she'd just done.

"Please," Holly begged. "We still haven't competed in a show together. I can't wait to see you whip Whitney in the Junior Open Jumping. Beating her will be the best way you can get back at her."

"Why don't *you* enter it instead of me," Kerry said. "You can beat her."

Holly shook her head. "Uh-uh. I chose Gambler's Choice, and it's too late to change my entry." She grasped Kerry's hand. "You've got to do it for yourself as well as Mom. If you back down now, you might not get another chance to beat Whitney Myers."

Kerry's heart started beating loudly. She felt torn into little pieces. Part of her wanted to ride in the show and beat Whitney once and for all, but the other part wanted to run away and hide from her problems. She wished her father would come home. She really needed him right now.

"I'll think about it," she finally agreed.

"Good. Let's go to the barn and practice some more," Holly said hopefully. "We've only got a few more days till the show, and I need to work on the flat. I entered that Equitation class, and I don't want to make a fool of myself."

Kerry tried to drum up some enthusiasm for riding, but it wasn't easy. All she wanted to do was cuddle Tapestry and hide from the rest of the world. As she buried her head in her horse's neck, she tried to remember everything that Mr. Hoffman had said. Suddenly she remembered his words—"as soon as I see her in action, I'll know for sure . . ."

Puzzled, she wondered what he meant. She thought

96

about it while she and Holly practiced in the outdoor riding ring. Whitney and Sue Armstrong were there as well. Kerry purposely kept out of Whitney's way. She didn't trust herself not to strangle the girl!

But Mr. Hoffman's strange words kept running around inside her head like an annoying mosquito. It didn't make any sense. How could he tell for sure about Tapestry just by watching her "in action"?

When she mentioned it to Holly later that afternoon, Holly shrugged, looking as baffled as she was.

But Kerry couldn't get it out of her mind. What was the mystery about Tapestry's "action"? Did she have some peculiar way of going over a jump that Mr. Hoffman would recognize, or was she skittish about horse show crowds? Kerry couldn't figure it out, and neither Liz nor Holly were any help at all.

Liz put her arm around Kerry's shoulders. "I know how hard you've worked with that horse, and I'm very proud of you. But you've got to face facts. If Tapestry really is Mr. Hoffman's horse, you have to give her back. It's the right thing to do. After all, if it weren't for you, Tapestry would be . . ." Her voice trailed off.

Kerry knew what she was going to say, and it was an ugly thought. She tried to pull herself together and be mature about everything. Dissolving in another flood of tears wasn't going to solve her dilemma. If Tapestry proved she was Mr. Hoffman's horse, Kerry knew she'd have to give her up gracefully. It would be the hardest thing she'd ever have to do, but it was the only way. Crying and causing a fuss would only make it worse. Still, it didn't help the pain she felt inside. It was like a sharp knife pricking at her heart, and it wouldn't go away.

On the way to the horse show, all the kids in the horse van talked nonstop at the tops of their voices. All except Kerry. She sat silently between Holly and Liz, miserably wrapped up in her own thoughts. While Sue, Robin, and Jennifer bounced around the back seat, all she could think about was her last day with Tapestry. She'd spent hours the night before, sitting in the mare's stall, thinking about letting her go. She knew she had to ride for the team and not let Liz down. The more she thought about it, the more determined she became to beat Whitney Myers. Even if she couldn't keep Tapestry forever, the least she could do was try her best to win.

As the van bounced along the rutted driveway leading to the showgrounds, Kerry looked idly out the window. Behind the two riding rings she could see several large tents and an enormous Ferris wheel. The horse show was part of the county fair, and already crowds of people had gathered to enjoy the festivities.

Liz parked the van, and the girls got busy unloading their horses. Jennifer and Robin ran off to get the team's numbers, and Liz told Holly and Whitney to get ready for their first class. They would be competing against each other in the Equitation class.

Angela, who'd arrived with Whitney and Mrs. Myers, leaned against the horse van and watched as Whitney put Astronaut's saddle on. "Are you going for the blue?" she asked with a sly grin.

Whitney tossed her head and looked scornfully in Holly's direction. "Of course! I'll win easily."

Holly muttered something under her breath and swung her leg over Magician's back. "Wish me luck," she said to Kerry before riding off to the waiting area. "I'm going to need it."

Holly's class was large—over twenty riders—and as Kerry leaned against the rails, she almost forgot the cloud hanging over her head. Magician looked superb. With Holly sitting tall and straight in the saddle, he trotted and cantered around without putting a foot wrong. Kerry felt sure they'd place in the top six. Holly was an outstanding rider; and in this class, it was her riding ability that was being judged.

The judge ordered all the competitors to line up in the center of the ring. Holly was too far away for Kerry to see her face clearly, but she could imagine what her friend was feeling—nervous and scared!

One by one each rider performed a figure eight and then trotted in a straight line toward the judge. Whitney's figure was sloppy; and when she trotted down the center of the ring, her toes were sticking out at right angles.

"Not an impressive performance," Liz said. "Let's hope Holly does better."

Kerry knew Liz was worried about Holly's first show since her accident. It was important for her confidence that she do well in this class. Otherwise, her nerve might be shot for the more difficult one ahead of her.

Holly's figure eight was almost flawless, and she

earned scattered applause from the audience.

For a few moments the judge conferred with the ring steward, and Kerry held her breath. In a few minutes the results were announced. She bit back a cry of disappointment when she heard the announcer inform them that the winner was a rider from Larchwood Equestrian Club. But her face broke into a broad smile as the judge pinned the second-place red ribbon onto Magician's bridle.

Liz started to cheer. "Well done!" she cried loudly as Holly trotted out of the ring with the red ribbon fluttering from Magician's bridle.

As Kerry ran up to her, Whitney thundered by on Astronaut. Her face was contorted into an angry scowl. There was no colorful ribbon decorating her horse's bridle. She hadn't even placed!

"That was terrific, Holly!" Kerry said. In all the excitement it was easy to forget her own troubles. "You must be thrilled."

Holly slipped off Magician's back and wrapped her arms around his neck. "You wonderful horse!" she said happily.

"Whitney didn't get pinned," Kerry muttered.

Holly groaned. "I know. She'll be impossible for the rest of the day. And I bet her mother's furious with her, too."

"Hey, Kerry, don't waste time," Liz said urgently. "You're in the Pleasure Horse class next."

Liz's words brought Kerry back down to earth. She looked around for any sign of Mr. Hoffman and his horse trailer, but so far, he hadn't shown up.

Kerry had to force herself to get ready for her class.

She knew Liz was counting on her to do well. The team was in third place at this point. Larchwood Equestrian Club, the leaders, were thirty points ahead, and Kerry knew they'd have to work hard to catch up.

Quietly she tried to clear her mind of everything except the event ahead of her. She followed Sue and Tara into the ring while Holly, Liz, Robin, and Jennifer stood at the rails and wished them luck. The class was almost as big as Holly's, and Kerry didn't think she stood much of a chance. All the other horses looked so gorgeous, she didn't envy the judge having to choose the winner.

Kerry concentrated on getting Tapestry to perform smoothly and quietly. She knew that was what the judge looked for in a pleasure horse—one that the judge himself would actually like to ride for pleasure.

When she was one of the six finalists chosen to perform an individual workout, Kerry was thrilled. For a moment she forgot all about Mr. Hoffman as she trotted and cantered in circles before the judge. Tapestry performed beautifully. With her nose tucked in and her tail held proudly, the good-looking mare swept around the ring to enthusiastic applause from the Timber Ridge crowd.

Finally the results were announced, and Kerry left the ring with the red ribbon. Just like Holly, she'd won second place, but her feeling of pride was tinged with a deep sadness. She only had one more chance to win a ribbon for her riding team before . . . She banished the thought. The only way she was going to get through the rest of the day was if she stopped torturing herself with thoughts of Mr. Hoffman.

Sue Armstrong, riding Tara, placed fourth in the Pleasure Class, and Liz was delighted. She checked her notes quickly. "I think we may have moved up to second place, thanks to you kids. You both rode very well."

Clutching her white ribbon, Sue hurried off to get ready for the trail class in the other ring. She only had ten minutes between classes. As soon as Kerry and Holly had settled Tapestry back in the horse van beside Magician, they went to watch Sue's class.

Sue and Tara pushed Timber Ridge ahead even further with a first-place ribbon. Liz was all smiles when the victorious pair cantered out of the ring. "Well done!" she cried happily. "Keep this up, kids, and we're going to win!"

While Holly got ready for the Gambler's Choice, Kerry kept a sharp lookout for Mr. Hoffman. But so far he hadn't shown up. She started to hope that he'd changed his mind, but knew she was being ridiculous. He said he was going to come and get his horse, and it made her feel sick just thinking about it.

"Are you sure you've got your course memorized?" Liz asked Holly as she helped her into the saddle.

Holly nodded. "Yup, I think so. I explained it all to Magician, and if I forget—it's up to him!"

Liz smiled and patted the horse's rump. "Don't push too hard, Holly. Remember. This is your first show, and you're still not as strong as you used to be."

Holly crammed her hard hat firmly on her head,

gathered up her reins, and rode into the ring. At the sound of the bell, she was off. In a flash Magician pounded between the starting posts and flew over the first fence. Then Holly swung him around an impossibly tight turn, and in two strides, they leaped over the parallel bars.

The astonished audience gasped in unison. No other rider had even attempted that particular maneuver, and it had put Holly seconds ahead of everyone else. She galloped over the next three jumps and was making an extraordinarily good time.

"She's crazy!" Liz exclaimed when Holly suddenly whipped her horse around and faced him at the in-and-out. "She'll never make it from there!"

Kerry held her breath and crossed her fingers. Holly had taken a huge risk—only giving Magician three strides to prepare for the tricky double jump. He ought to have had more of a run at it in order to get over both jumps properly. But the magnificent horse rose to the occasion and cleared them both.

"Phew," Kerry exhaled slowly and glanced at the timing clock.

"She might win if she keeps this up," Liz said quietly.

There had only been four other clear rounds, and none as fast as Holly's. Now if only she can get over the last two jumps, Kerry thought.

Holly and Magician thundered toward the five-bar gate. Just before the take-off, Magician skidded and almost swerved away from the fence. But Holly checked him in time and guided him over it without a mishap. One more fence and she had it made!

Tension settled over the crowd as the girl on the big black horse approached the forbidding red wall. One . . . two . . . three, Kerry counted silently as Magician's bounding strides drew him closer to the last obstacle. With a gigantic leap, he threw himself forward.

The crowd gasped as one of his hind feet touched the top row of bricks. "Oh, no!" Kerry cried. "It's going to fall!"

The brick wobbled precariously on top of the wall, and as Magician landed on the other side, Kerry shut her eyes. She couldn't watch. Suddenly the crowd burst into a frenzy of clapping, and she knew it was over. The brick hadn't fallen, and Holly and Magician went careening madly between the finish posts.

"She did it!" Liz cried. "She went clear!"

A few minutes later a triumphant Holly rode out of the ring with the victorious blue ribbon pinned to her horse. "Mom, we won!" she yelled at the top of her voice.

While everyone crowded around, showering Holly with congratulations, Kerry tensed up. A tall thin man was making his way toward them, and if she wasn't mistaken, it was Mr. Hoffman.

Chapter Twelve

"Hello, everyone."

Kerry slipped quietly away with Mr. Hoffman's greeting ringing in her ears. No one saw her as she ran back toward the Timber Ridge horse van. She didn't want to face Mr. Hoffman yet. She wasn't ready. She needed more time alone with Tapestry first.

Once inside the van's cool interior, Kerry collapsed onto a bale of hay and tried to clear her head. Tapestry, tied up next to her in one of the stalls, nudged her gently with her soft muzzle.

"I can't help it," Kerry cried softly. "I feel so awful."

There was no one to share her anguish with—no one except Tapestry. The other horses and riders were still outside congratulating Holly on her victory.

Kerry took a deep breath and tried to analyze her predicament. Mr. Hoffman had said Tapestry/Melody was a good show horse. What if she purposely fouled up in the jumping class? It wouldn't take much effort—all she had to do was place the mare wrong at the jumps, or keep too tight a rein on her. Tapestry would probably knock everything down, and then Mr. Hoffman would say she wasn't his horse after all. Not if she messed up really badly with her in the show ring.

She pondered that option for a moment or two. It might work! Then she thought about her overriding desire to beat Whitney once and for all. And there were Liz's hopes for winning the team trophy. And maybe most important was her loyalty to Tapestry herself—it would be a betrayal to the horse to make her look like anything less than what she was. Kerry knew she couldn't go through with it. No. She had to force herself to face reality. She had to grow up and accept Tapestry's departure gracefully.

Kerry wound her arms around Tapestry's neck and tried to ignore the pain she was feeling inside. In a few hours she'd have her last ride on Tapestry—a ride that would seal Tapestry's fate! And then Tapestry would leave, and all she'd be left with was a warm, wonderful memory of her first horse.

"I'll never forget you," Kerry whispered into Tapestry's silky mane. "Wherever I go, and whatever I do, you'll be with me always."

Feeling a little better for having made what she knew was the right decision, Kerry felt able to go outside and join the rest of the world. Her jumping class—her chance to beat Whitney—was only an hour away, and she knew she had to psych herself up for the challenge.

Whitney made it easy for her. "I'll make mincemeat out of you in that class!" she jeered as Kerry rejoined the group around Holly and Magician.

Kerry glared at her. "No, you won't. I've been waiting all summer to beat you, Whitney Myers, and I'm going to do just that!"

"Easily," Holly added.

"Kerry, Mr. Hoffman stopped by," Liz interrupted over the girls' loud voices. "He said to tell you he'd be back in time for your jumping class."

Kerry was relieved that she wouldn't have to talk to him before she went in the ring. She was having a hard enough time as it was coping with Whitney's sneers and snide remarks—to say nothing of battling her own inner feelings.

As calmly as she could, Kerry studied the course map. The jumps were set at about three feet, and some of them had enormous spreads to them. The double oxer—a set of three poles, the middle one higher than the two outer ones—had a very wide spread to it. There were the usual parallel bars, a five-bar gate, and the ever-present red brick wall, along with a style, barrels, a brush jump, and a coop. Kerry grinned briefly at the thought of jumping the coop. It really did look like an old wooden chicken coop, and she hoped Tapestry wouldn't shy away from it. She'd never jumped one with her before.

There were eight fences, and the course was full of twists and turns. Kerry hoped there wouldn't be a jump-off. If two or more riders were tied at the end of the competition, they'd have to jump again. This time, against the clock. The fastest one would win.

She spent the next forty-five minutes getting Tapestry ready for her big moment. At first she trotted and cantered slowly in a wide circle, loosening the mare's muscles and getting her to bend and flex at the neck. Then she took her over the two small practice jumps beside the main jumping ring. The class had already started, but so far none of the other competitors had had clear rounds.

Whitney rode up on Astronaut. "I want to practice," Whitney said loudly. "Are you finished?"

Kerry slowed Tapestry down to a walk. "Go ahead," she said shortly. There was no point in jumping her horse any more. Tapestry was already warmed up and raring to go.

She sat and watched as Whitney cantered her big bay horse over the jumps. Astronaut was going well. He was an excellent jumper, and he'd gotten over his foul mood of the previous week. Kerry knew she was going to have to ride extremely well in order to beat them.

Whitney looked very pleased with herself when she finished. She cantered up to Kerry, a superior smile on her face. "You don't stand a chance against me," she stated coolly. "Why don't you just back down? You'll only make a fool of yourself!"

Her words only inflamed Kerry's desire to beat her. Victory over Whitney would be a fitting farewell for Tapestry before she left with Mr. Hoffman. Kerry was determined to do everything she could to make it come true.

Just then Liz ran up to them. "We're looking good. If you kids can get twenty points between you in this class, we'll win the team trophy."

"How many points does the winner get?" Whitney asked nonchalantly as if she already had the blue ribbon in the bag.

Liz consulted the clipboard in her hand. "Twenty."

"No problem," Whitney said confidently. "I'm going to win, and no one's going to stop me!"

As she rode off, Liz shook her head. "Just take it easy out there, Kerry. A second and third place between you will do it, too. That'll add up to the points we need."

Kerry promised to do her best. Then she tried to relax as her turn to jump drew closer. Whitney went into the ring before she did. Kerry held her breath as Astronaut cleared one fence after another in perfect form. He didn't put a foot wrong, and Whitney ended up with the first clear round of the Junior Open Jumping.

"See, what did I tell you!" she said scornfully as she came out of the ring. "I'm going to win!"

Kerry's nerve almost faltered. The only way she could beat Whitney now was to get a clear round as well. Then they'd have to face each other in a timed jump-off. Memories of the Hampshire Classic, where she'd allowed Whitney to win the blue ribbon, flooded through her mind. This time she wouldn't back down and let Whitney win by default. This time she'd beat her!

"Good luck!" Holly yelled when the bell rang, signaling Kerry's turn to ride.

Kerry adjusted her hard hat, tightened her grip on the saddle, and trotted into the ring. Just before

110

the judge waved his flag for her to begin her round, she caught sight of Mr. Hoffman walking up to Holly. So he'd made it back in time. She fought down a feeling of nausea. This wasn't the time to back out and mess things up. She had to concentrate. Hard.

The course of colorful jumps looked enormous. As Kerry approached the brush jump, she hoped she wouldn't suddenly forget the route she had to take. If she did, she'd be eliminated.

A hush settled over the audience as Tapestry took off over the brush jump. Bright waves of sunlight danced off the mare's copper-colored hindquarters, and her silvery mane and tail streamed out behind her as she leaped gracefully over the jump.

As soon as Tapestry's forelegs hit the ground, Kerry eased her in a gentle right turn to face the style. It was a very narrow jump, and she almost scraped her foot against one of the uprights as Tapestry cleared it.

Since she wasn't being timed, Kerry took her time pulling Tapestry around to face the chicken coop. It was painted bright yellow, and it had a red and white pole on top. "Easy now, girl," she whispered into Tapestry's flying mane. She leaned forward, urging the mare to increase her stride.

For a few seconds she felt Tapestry falter. She obviously didn't like the alien obstacle in front of her. Kerry squeezed hard with her legs and gave the mare her head. Tapestry responded and leaped over the coop.

As they landed, Kerry wondered if Mr. Hoffman was watching. Was Tapestry somehow proving to him that she was his missing horse? She quickly banished him from her mind and looked toward the next jump. Carefully she steered Tapestry around a tight corner and approached the parallel bars.

"One . . . two . . . three," Kerry said to herself as Tapestry took off.

Clunk!

"Oh, no!" Kerry cried as one of Tapestry's forelegs rapped the jump. It was going to fall.

While the mare's body was arced over the jump, Kerry held her breath. She glanced down as the blur of poles and ground zoomed by beneath her. The pole was rocking back and forth in its metal holder, but it didn't fall.

The crowd cheered as Kerry cantered toward the double oxer.

Tapestry's ears flicked back and forth, and Kerry checked her. This jump had a wide spread, and she didn't want to land in the middle of it because she misjudged the fence.

When Tapestry was only three strides away, Kerry let her go. The mare leaped forward eagerly and soared over the double oxer with an enormous leap. Only three more fences to go, and they'd be home clear!

Tapestry jumped the five-bar gate without a moment's hesitation, and then Kerry swung her into a hard left-hand turn to go over the barrels. She misjudged the distance. As Tapestry was about to take off, Kerry was sure she'd blown it. They were too close to the jump. Tapestry couldn't possibly clear it!

She almost cried with relief when the mare twisted her body over the fence and somehow landed safely.

"You fantastic horse!" Kerry cried. She looked ahead of her. Only the wall was left, and it looked enormous!

The crowd started cheering as she approached the last jump in the course. "Go on, girl, you can do it!" Kerry cried.

She felt Tapestry's mane whipping into her face as she moved her body forward. The mare raced toward the red brick jump and took off.

But it was too soon. Kerry was expecting Tapestry to take another stride. They'd never get over the wall!

The crowd cried "Ooohhhhh!" Kerry felt as if she were taking off into outer space. Tapestry leaped up and forward, her graceful body curving over the jump, with Kerry crouched low over her neck.

Thud! They landed safely on the other side to an enthusiastic round of cheering and applause. Kerry left the ring with the announcer's words ringing in her ears. "Another clear round, ladies and gentlemen. Will the next rider . . ."

Kerry's joy and elation were short-lived. She'd no sooner jumped off Tapestry's back and flung her arms around the mare's neck when Holly and Mr. Hoffman ran up to her.

This was it. The moment when she'd know for sure what Tapestry's fate was going to be. She took a deep breath and told herself to be mature. She wouldn't cry. She wouldn't.

"Kerry, that was fantastic!" Holly yelled. "And you're not gonna believe this, but—"

Mr. Hoffman cut her off. "Let me tell her, please."

"Tell me what?" Kerry looked at him suspiciously.

He'd gotten what he wanted. Tapestry was his. She wasn't going to make a fuss. What more did he have to say to her?

"I owe you a huge apology," Mr. Hoffman said gently as he patted Tapestry's sweaty neck. "I'm afraid I've put you through a load of agony for nothing. I'm sorry."

"Huh?" Kerry asked. "What do you mean?"

"This isn't my mare," Mr. Hoffman said quietly.

At first Kerry thought she'd misheard him. Surely he wasn't saying the exact words she wanted to hear. It couldn't be true . . . could it?

She looked at Holly's smiling face. "You can believe it," Holly said. "Tapestry isn't Melody. Isn't that fantastic?"

Kerry's legs gave out from underneath her, and she sank into a heap on the ground. "I don't believe it. Are you sure? How can you be sure?"

"I'm sure," he replied wistfully, still staring at Tapestry. "I wish she were mine, but she isn't."

Kerry felt like crying with relief. "But how could you tell?"

Mr. Hoffman gave an embarrassed cough. "I was ninety-nine percent sure that your horse was Melody, but I had to see her again to be one hundred percent sure. You see, Melody had a peculiar habit," Mr. Hoffman explained. "She had this strange way of flicking her tail to one side when she went over a jump. It was something we used to joke about. But your mare doesn't do that, and that's how I know. I'm sorry to have put you through all this."

Kerry sat on the ground, stunned by the good

news. So that's what he meant by seeing her in action. If only she'd had the time to jump Tapestry that day he came to the barn. Then she wouldn't have had to endure the agony of waiting and wondering for the past few weeks.

"Oh, Tapestry, I get to keep you," she murmured when the mare put her nose down and nudged her.

Liz ran up, full of congratulations. She'd already heard the good news about Tapestry and her face was all smiles. "Come on, Kerry. You'll be in the jump-off. Two other kids had clear rounds, so it's up to you and Whitney to do your best." She looked at Kerry's smiling face. "Think you're up to it?"

"You bet!" Kerry said quickly. "Now I know for sure I can keep Tapestry, I'd jump the grandstand if you asked me to!"

Whitney and Astronaut rode by on their way to the collecting ring. "Your clear round was just a fluke," Whitney said. "You'll never make it round the course faster than me!"

Kerry gritted her teeth. Now she knew she was going to win. She had to. She'd never forgive herself if she let Whitney beat her. Victory was so close she could almost taste it.

The ring stewards raised the height of several jumps, and the timing clock was turned on. The four riders in the jump-off had only five fences to jump— the style, parallel bars, double oxer, the barrels, and the red wall. They all drew straws to see who would jump first. Kerry didn't know if she was relieved or not when she found out that she would be the first one in the ring.

"Remember, if you take it carefully and get a clear round, you stand a better chance than if you rush it," Liz warned as Kerry put her foot in the stirrup. "Don't watch the clock. Just concentrate on a clear round."

Kerry forgot about everyone and everything as soon as the bell rang. Tapestry charged through the starting posts and headed toward the style. As soon as they'd cleared it, Kerry pulled her sharply around to the left, giving her only four strides to get over the parallel bars. It was an enormous risk. She probably ought to have turned right, gone around the style and given herself a better run at the next jump. But this way was quicker.

She held her breath as Tapestry skidded on take-off. Maybe she'd just ruined her chances.

But the valiant chestnut mare righted herself and scraped over the parallel bars without knocking them down. Kerry let out a sigh of relief and galloped toward the double oxer, keeping a careful eye on the fence beyond it. She was going to risk another tight turn.

They leaped over the double oxer, and Kerry steered the mare into a sharp right turn. Two strides, and they leaped over the barrels. Tapestry's forelegs had no sooner hit the ground when Kerry pulled her around to the left and kicked her hard.

Tapestry responded, even though she was tired. It was as if she knew how important this was to Kerry. She bounded eagerly toward the brick wall. The crowd started cheering again. Kerry could sense they were making an incredibly good time.

117

"Don't blow it!" she warned herself. Too often, overconfident show jumpers ruined their chances at the last fence.

"Careful now," she muttered as the wall drew closer. She leaned forward as Tapestry took off. It was a magical feeling—soaring upward on her very own horse! One that she'd rescued from certain death and turned into a champion show jumper.

"Hooray!" she heard Holly and Liz yelling as she and Tapestry landed on the other side and raced between the finish posts.

She'd gone clear, and a glance at the clock told her that she'd done it in forty-three seconds!

The next finalist, one of the Larchwood riders, trotted past her, ready to begin his ride. Kerry cantered into the collecting ring and almost fell off her horse in surprise.

There, standing not ten feet in front of her, was . . . Kerry blinked twice and looked again. It couldn't be, could it?

With a loud shriek she flung herself off Tapestry's back and hurled herself into the man's outstretched arms. "Dad! Dad!" Kerry cried. "When did you get here? I thought you weren't coming home till the fall!"

Ben Logan lifted his daughter off her feet and swung her around. "I got here just in time to see that fantastic ride, young lady. Well done, that was a terrific performance!"

Kerry buried her head in his shoulder. His navy blazer smelled of his favorite cologne, and when his beard tickled her face, she pulled away. "I almost didn't recognize you. When did you grow all that hair on your face?" The last time she'd seen him at the beginning of the summer, he was clean-shaven.

Her father laughed and hugged her again. "Like it?"

Kerry studied him carefully, noting the deeply tanned face above the gray-streaked beard. His blue-gray eyes had laugh lines in the corners, and he looked more handsome than ever. "You look great!" she said happily.

Suddenly Tapestry tugged at the reins, jogging Kerry's arm. "Dad, this is Tapestry. Isn't she the most wonderful horse in the world?"

Gently he untangled himself from Kerry's arms and listened as she introduced him to her new horse. His cheerful expression changed to a more solemn one, and Kerry was instantly alarmed. After all this, suppose he wanted her to sell Tapestry?

"Dad, you do like her, don't you? I can keep her?" Kerry's voice cracked with apprehension.

"Not so fast, Kerry," her father replied, still looking closely at the chestnut mare. "We've got a lot of catching up to do, so let's just take things one at a time."

"But, Dad!" Kerry protested. She didn't like the tone of his voice. It didn't sound too encouraging. "Please let me keep her, please! I'll work to pay for her keep, I'll do anything! Please say yes."

"Kerry, she's a beautiful horse, but I can't make any promises. Not yet. I don't know where my next job assignment's going to be." Then he smiled and put his arm around Kerry's shoulders. "Look, I promise I'll do what I can for you, but this is something we have to talk about later. Not now. Besides, I think someone's trying to get your attention."

Kerry turned around. Liz was running toward her. "Hey, Liz!" Kerry yelled. "Guess who's here?"

Liz's astonishment at meeting Ben Logan was even greater than Kerry's. After a hurried introduction she filled Kerry in on what had been happening in the jumping ring. "So far, you're in the lead, Kerry. One of the others got ten faults, and the other was clear, but slower than you."

Just then Whitney cantered past them on her way to the jumping ring. Kerry held her breath as Whitney galloped over the first jump. Then she did exactly what Kerry had done—cut a sharp corner to take the parallel bars. Astronaut cleared the jump magnificently, and Kerry glanced at the time clock. They were going around fast. Very fast!

Horse and rider flew over the double oxer, and then the barrels without a mistake, and the clock showed thirty-five seconds. I can't bear to watch! Kerry thought miserably. She shut her eyes as Whitney approached the wall. The suspense was killing her.

Crack!

Kerry opened her eyes in time to see Astronaut demolishing the red brick wall. Whitney had mistimed the take-off, and her horse blundered right through the jump. Wooden bricks scattered everywhere as Astronaut struggled to extricate himself from the wall.

"You've won!" Holly cried. "You've finally beaten her. You've beaten Whitney Myers!"

Suddenly Kerry was surrounded by people, all

talking and laughing at once, Holly the loudest of all. "I knew you could do it!" she shouted.

Ben Logan smiled proudly as everyone congratulated his daughter. "I'm sure glad I got here in time for this," he said to her. "I wouldn't have missed it for anything!"

Kerry's heart warmed to his praise. But inside a little voice warned her not to get too excited. He still hadn't said she could keep Tapestry, and she knew better than to ask again. She'd have to wait until the time was right. But she was sure that once he got to know Tapestry like she did, he'd give in. Somehow they'd find a way to keep her horse.

In all the noise and confusion Kerry felt someone tugging at her arm. "Come on, dummy! We won the trophy! They're calling us into the ring."

In a daze she allowed Holly to drag her toward the judge in the middle of the jumping arena. Whitney and Sue ran ahead of them. Liz and Ben Logan remained by the rails and cheered loudly as the judge gave each rider a red, white, and blue ribbon. The cheers grew even louder when Kerry was awarded the first-place blue ribbon for the Junior Open Jumping. Whitney, her face flushed and angry, grudgingly accepted her third-place yellow ribbon.

Then the judge took the enormous silver trophy from the ring steward and looked inquiringly at the four young riders in front of him. "Which one of you is going to take this?"

Whitney immediately stepped forward, but Holly grabbed her arm and stopped her. "No, you don't!" she said fiercely.

Whitney turned around angrily. "Let go of me!" she snapped.

Holly ignored her and pushed Kerry forward. "You take it," she said firmly. "You're the one who deserves it."

A tremendous feeling of accomplishment flooded through Kerry as she shyly took the challenge trophy from the smiling judge. In that moment she knew that all her dreams had finally come true. She'd proved to everyone that she was right when she'd rescued Tapestry from the auction, and best of all, her father had come home in time to share in her triumph.

The crowd clapped and cheered as Kerry and Holly walked out of the ring arm in arm, proudly carrying the trophy between them. Whitney, with an ugly scowl on her face, disappeared as soon as they reached the collecting ring.

"You finally beat her," Holly said with a wicked grin. "How does it feel?"

"Fantastic!" Kerry replied. She touched the trophy and admired her ribbons—a blue one for winning the jumping, red for placing second, and the tri-color team ribbon.

"What did your dad say about Tapestry?" Holly asked. "Will he let you keep her?"

Kerry shrugged. "I hope so," she said slowly. "I think he likes her, but it all depends on his next job. I don't know where we're going to live."

Holly looked thoughtful for a moment. "Hey," she said slowly, "wouldn't it be great if you could both come and live at Timber Ridge?"

Kerry sighed and shook her head. "How I wish!"

Holly grinned and ran off. As Kerry watched her

friend's blond hair bouncing up and down, she thought about what Holly had just suggested. What a terrific idea! If only she and her father could move to Timber Ridge. That way she wouldn't have to say good-by to her best friend.

As Kerry walked toward her horse, she allowed herself to dream. Thoughts of her father and her settling into a pretty little house at Timber Ridge flashed through her mind. Surely her father could find a different job—one that didn't require he travel all over the world! That way they could live near Holly and Liz, and keep Tapestry at the stables!

She ran her hand down Tapestry's neck, then encircled the mare's soft muzzle with her arms. Burying her face into Tapestry's mane, she sighed aloud. "If only my dream could come true," she said softly.

Tapestry whinnied and nudged her owner gently.

"You understand, don't you?" Kerry cried. "Oh, I love you so much, Tapestry. I think you're the most wonderful horse in the world."

"You used to say that about Magician," Holly's voice said right behind her.

Kerry grinned and turned around. "Okay, they're *both* the most wonderful horses in the world!"

"And you're the best friend I've ever had," Holly said gently.

"We'll be friends forever," Kerry added quickly. "No matter what happens, right?"

"Right," Holly agreed. "Best friends forever!"